"What can I do to help make you un-cranky? Need ice cream? Gummy bears? Are pickles still popular with pregnant women?"

Grinning, shaking her head, Gabby said, "You'd better be glad I'm stuck in this bed, or that comment would earn you a pillow beating."

"Sounds hot," Dane teased, infuriating her all the more. "But seriously, anything you need done as far as getting ready for the baby? Tell me. I'll make it happen."

"Thank you." She wanted to meet his gaze, but couldn't.

"What's wrong?" Too late—he'd not only seen, but edged farther up the bed. His big hand now rested atop Gabby's belly. Heat licked through her, warring with her already heightened senses.

What was wrong? Try everything! It was against every law of nature for her to be turned on by Ben's brother.

Or was it?

Dear Reader,

While every story I write contains at least a smidge of my true life, *A Wedding for Baby* has more than usual. Like Gabby, I was on total bed rest while carrying my twins. Only, I started the process much earlier than she did! At my two-month checkup, my doctor announced my blood pressure was dangerously high, and voilà, I went from an exciting career in interior design to being a full-time "bed potato."

It's funny, but at the time, being waited on by my husband, grandma and grandpa, mom and dad, along with a half-dozen amazing neighbors, felt more like punishment than pleasure. I'd dreamed of a so-called normal pregnancy. Hours spent decorating the nursery and shopping for teeny-tiny socks. Instead, for months I sobbed to *The Waltons* reruns, did counted cross-stitch and ate *everything!* LOL!

Sixteen years after the fact, I look back on the time with great fondness. Never had I experienced such an outpouring of love. Never had I been more aware and grateful of belonging to a wonderful family. It is my hope that Gabby and Dane's story fills you with the same special family warmth.

Happy reading!

Laura Marie

A Wedding for Baby
LAURA MARIE ALTOM

HARLEQUIN®

TORONTO • NEW YORK • LONDON
AMSTERDAM • PARIS • SYDNEY • HAMBURG
STOCKHOLM • ATHENS • TOKYO • MILAN • MADRID
PRAGUE • WARSAW • BUDAPEST • AUCKLAND

Recycling programs
for this product may
not exist in your area.

ISBN-13: 978-0-373-75280-5

A WEDDING FOR BABY

Copyright © 2009 by Laura Marie Altom.

www.eHarlequin.com

Printed in U.S.A.

ABOUT THE AUTHOR

After college (Go, Hogs!), bestselling, award-winning author Laura Marie Altom did a brief stint as an interior designer before becoming a stay-at-home mom to boy/girl twins and a bonus son. Always an avid romance reader, she knew it was time to try her hand at writing when she found herself replotting the afternoon soaps.

When not immersed in her next story, Laura teaches art at a local middle school. In her free time she beats her kids at video games, tackles Mount Laundry and of course reads romance!

Laura loves hearing from readers at either P.O. Box 2074, Tulsa, OK 74101, or e-mail, BaliPalm@aol.com.

Love winning fun stuff? Check out lauramariealtom.com!

Books by Laura Marie Altom

HARLEQUIN AMERICAN ROMANCE

*U.S. Marshals

*The dedication for the book was purchased
as a fundraiser for Tulsa Memorial Cheer!
Thank you, **Mary Brandt,** for helping to
send our girls to Nationals! Go, Chargers!*

To my Mom and Dad…
I love you both and thank you for everything!

To my son Richard…
You are remarkable! I love you, son!

To my son Curtis…
Believe and it will be true! I love you, son!

To Lindsay…
Thank you for finding the man of your dreams
and becoming a part of this family!

To my sister, Denise…
You are truly one of the greatest people I know!

To my brother, Stacy…
Love and peace to you, Taddy Bum!

And to Stephen, I love you, babe!

Chapter One

"Contemplating making a run for it?"

Startled, Gabby Craig looked out of her open driver's-side window to find the last person on the planet she wanted to see. The Honorable Judge Dane Bocelli—Ben's big brother.

"You're allowed, you know? Hell, if they weren't my flesh and blood, I'd be home watching football."

"Go away, Dane. I'm actually very much looking forward to sharing Sunday supper with your family."

"That why you've been sitting in this heat, staring straight ahead for the past five minutes?"

"You timed me?" She'd been so deep in thought that she hadn't even noticed him pulling up behind her.

"Not intentionally. I've been waiting to help you from your car. You are about eighteen months pregnant with Ben's baby. It can't be easy. Going it alone."

"I manage," she snapped, grabbing her purse and a plate of cookies from the passenger seat. Seeing how the quiet, maple-lined street in the heart of Valley View's historic district was hardly a hotbed of crime, she took her keys from the ignition but left her windows down. She attempted opening her door, but was mortified to find that with both hands full and her huge belly crammed against the wheel, she did indeed need assistance.

"Let me take all of that," Dane said, opening her door and then taking her purse, keys and foil-wrapped plate. He tossed her keys in her purse and slung the leather bag over his left forearm, shifting the cookies to his left hand. He held out his right hand to her. "Ready?"

"Thank you," Gabby said to be polite, even though she really didn't want this man's help. Or a whiff of his rich, citrus-and-leather cologne. Everything about Dane was imposing. His towering height and powerful build. His being nearly ten years older than her. His penchant for dark suits paired with red power ties. The judge's perma-scowl that even across the Bocelli Sunday family dinner table usually left her feeling *guilty*. Throw in short-cropped dark hair, somber brown eyes and voilà— Dane was the polar opposite of his always smiling, blue-eyed brother.

Out of the car, Gabby dropped Dane's hand as if it were electrified. In the year she and Ben had dated, in the six months since Ben had left her for greener pastures, Dane had never been overly kind. Never rude, but distant.

Ignoring her runaway pulse, she forced a deep breath.

"I've always loved your parents' house," she said, desperate to fill the awkward silence. The pink, green and white Queen Anne with its scalloped siding, elaborate trim and turret on the right side always made Gabby think of a wedding cake. Too pretty to eat, yet a creation she could gaze upon all day long. Throw in Mama Bocelli's famous flower gardens ringing the house and the place was a slice of fragrant heaven. She and Ben used to share the porch swing while his still-feisty grandmother entertained them with outrageous stories from her youth. Now the swing and white-wicker rockers sat empty, hanging baskets of ferns still in the stagnant Arkansas heat.

Dane shrugged. "This monstrosity is a maintenance nightmare."

"But worth it, right?" They crossed the street and stepped onto a winding brick sidewalk.

Dane's only response was another shrug.

Whatever. It wasn't as if she'd come here to see him. In fact, when Ben's mother had issued the invitation, Gabby had secretly hoped Dane wouldn't be in attendance.

"Look at you!" The front door had burst open and out came Mama Bocelli across the porch and down the stairs, arms outstretched for a hug. "You're glowing!"

Gabby grimaced. After looking in the mirror one last time before heading out, Gabby had been convinced she'd never looked worse.

Ben's mother hugged the way she cooked and gardened—with warmth and unabashed pleasure. The woman's heart was as big as her dyed-black hair. Gabby's throat unexpectedly swelled from the pleasure of being held—even by Ben's mother. With no family in town, her loneliness had at times been overwhelming.

"Girl," Mama said, still holding Gabby's hands but

stepping back to appraise her. "You're too thin. Let's get you inside for a solid meal."

Nana Bocelli tottered out the door and onto the porch. "Gabrielle, you're about the size of the Hendersons' new backyard storage shed!"

From behind, Dane laughed. "Nana, I was just thinking the same thing. Only she's a pleasing-looking shed."

"Dane!" Mama scolded. "What a horrible thing to say, and, Nana, I thought I asked you to keep an eye on the marinara sauce?"

Nana yawned. "I got bored."

Once Gabby had mounted the steps—Mama helping her every step of the way—Nana pulled her into another great hug. "It's been too long since we've seen you. You should stop by more often."

"I know," Gabby said, following along with the tide as they all ushered her inside. "Work has been crazy, and—"

"You should make time for family," Mama said.

Pops Bocelli was snoring in his favorite recliner.

Mama kicked it, but he just changed position.

Hiding a smile at the antics of the long-married couple, Gabby said, "I know, and I love thinking of you all as family, but with Ben out of my life, I don't want to intrude."

"Ben's a fool," Dane said, passing them on his way into the house.

"Ignore him," Mama urged. "Now, come and sit at the kitchen table while I finish up. I want to hear all about what you've been doing."

Dutifully complying, Gabby trailed after the buxom

woman. The kitchen's air was sumptuous. Laden with rich scents of simmering marinara and the lasagna's cheese. "Mmm..." she breathed in "—I've so missed your cooking."

"You're welcome anytime. I've told you that."

"Mama," Dane interjected from a shadowy corner, arms crossed. "Gabrielle and Ben are no longer together. It's only natural that she'd want her space."

"Stay out of it," his mother snapped. "Your brother will be back to marry this girl and raise their baby, and when he does, you'll eat your words."

Sighing, he said, "With all due respect, Mama, Ben's a different breed than the rest of us. To him, responsibility is a dirty word."

"Hush," Mama said, Nana watching on as if this was the best entertainment she'd had in weeks. "Gabrielle, would you like a glass of milk? Maybe juice?"

"No, thank you," she said, feeling caught up in the middle of a battle the family been waging most of Ben's life. As amazing as he was, he was also that infuriating.

Mama poured her a glass of milk anyway, setting it on the table, along with a cheese-filled Danish. "Here, you need a before-supper snack."

"Thank you," Gabby said, even though what she'd have really liked was a sampling of lasagna.

"Now," Mama said, "I was talking with Bella Marconi—you know, my canasta partner from down the street—and she said her pregnant daughter is about as far along as you and starting Lamaze. Have you checked into any classes?"

"Yes," Gabby said, "but you have to have a partner."

"I'm available most every night of the week," Nana said. "Except for Tuesdays. That's my and Edgar Rowley's regular date night."

"Um, Nana, thanks for the offer," Gabby said, "but I still have a week to find someone before my class starts."

Pouring Italian dressing onto baby greens, Mama said, "Don't you worry, honey. I'll put my thinking cap on and come up with the perfect partner."

AN HOUR LATER, MAMA SNAPPED her fingers and said, "Dane! He can be your partner! I can't believe I didn't think of it sooner." Gabby sucked a bite of lasagna down her windpipe, coughing till she nearly blacked out. The heat didn't help, seeing how Pops Bocelli was too cheap to turn on the central A.C. An oscillating fan stirred soupy air, moaning with each turn.

Nana patted her back. "You all right?"

"F-fine," Gabby finally managed to say.

Helping herself to thirds of lasagna, Nana made a slurping noise with her dentures. "Now that you're breathing again, I think Therese has an excellent idea. Don't you, Dane?"

"Um…"

"See?" Mama said, picking up the bread basket and thrusting it at Gabby. "My *good* boy agrees, don't you, Dane?"

Suddenly fascinated by his salad, he ducked his head.

"For God's sake, Therese," said Pops. "Leave it to Ben to clean up after himself."

"Clean up?" Mama slapped the lace-topped table hard enough to rattle the good china. Three red rose

petals drifted down from a center arrangement. "This is your future grandchild. If *your* son were half a man, he would marry the poor girl. Make an honest woman of her, but *nooo…*" She blew her nose into the embroidered handkerchief she kept stashed up her sleeve. "*Your* boy would rather break his mother's heart than—"

"Don't cry, Ma." Ben's big brother, an inch taller and a hundred times more responsible, said, "I'll do it."

"That's a dear boy." Nana patted his hand. She was a *patter*. To her way of thinking, there was no crisis too large or small that a simple pat could not make better. If only Gabby felt the same.

Far from it, she wanted to slide out of her chair and onto the floor, where she would then crawl unseen out of the house to run screaming down the street. She should've known better than to even mention Lamaze to Mama. But then wait, Mama had been the one who'd brought it up.

"You'll see," Pops said around a bite of his lasagna. "Ben'll do the right thing. Mark my words, Gabrielle, he'll not only be back in time for your Lamaze class, but to marry you. Give the baby our family name."

"Th-that's okay," she said, curving her hand over her bulging tummy. "I shouldn't have even said anything. I'll find someone else to be my Lamaze coach. Maybe a friend from—"

"I'll do it," Dane said. Was it anger darkening his tone? If so, was he put out with her? His mother? His little brother? Or could it be something else making him sound less than his usually unflappable, professional self?

"But, Dane," Gabby argued, "really, I'm sure one of my friends from work will be happy to—"

He fought right back. "I said, I'd—"

"No," she insisted. "I won't—"

An earsplitting whistle erupted from Nana. How the woman managed it with her dentures Gabby didn't know, but when it came to getting folks' attention, Nana got the job done. "Gabrielle, say thank-you to Dane. Dane—smile. Act like spending a few nights with your brother's pregnant future bride is an honor, rather than—"

"I'm not marrying Ben," Gabby protested.

"Hush!" Pops said. "All of this screeching is making my stomach sour." He clutched his chest.

Mama made clucking sounds, passing Pops the bread. "Eat more. It'll counteract the acid."

He nodded.

Dane rolled his eyes.

Nana upended a bottle of Chianti into her emptied milk cup.

"What are you doing?" Mama asked. "Your doctor said lay off the sauce."

Nana clicked her dentures before downing a big swig.

Under his breath, Dane asked Gabby, "Want to get out of here? Talk?"

She placed her napkin alongside her plate.

"What's wrong with talking here?" Pops asked. "Your mother made cake."

Dane stood, kissed the top of his mother's head. "We'll be back for dessert."

"Promise?" Mama asked.

"Oh, for crying out loud," Nana said, stealing Pops's wine, "he's a grown man, Therese. Let him have some fun."

"SORRY." IN A DINER THREE blocks from his parents' home, Dane leaned his head back and sighed. He and Gabrielle shared a black vinyl corner booth. Coffee and apple juice were on the way. Sinatra crooned from the jukebox. The daily chicken-and-dumpling special flavored blessedly cool air. The only other diners were two white-haired guys playing checkers at the counter. "Tonight got a little crazy."

"A *little?*" Gabby yanked a napkin from a chrome holder and proceeded to shred it into about fifty pieces. "I've never been more mortified in my life."

"Not even when my loser brother left you on your own and pregnant?" The second the words left Dane's mouth, he regretted them. Regretted the way she'd stopped shredding her napkin to instead grip the pieces so tightly her knuckles whitened. "Sorry, again. That came out wrong."

She shook her head. "You called it the way you see it. If the truth hurts…" She shrugged.

"Still…" He should've reached across the table, eased his fingers between hers and squeezed. Her complexion was pale and her eyes were wet; her lower lip almost imperceptibly trembled. A part of him was afraid she'd cry. Which would've been bad.

"Really," she said with a sniffle, "I'm over Ben's leaving."

"You don't look it."

Her gaping mouth told him yet again he should've kept his big mouth shut.

Luckily, the waitress arrived, placing their drinks on the table with little fanfare. "How far along are you?" she asked Gabrielle.

"A little over six months."

"Whew." With a faint smile, the waitress, whose name tag read *Candace,* added, "I don't envy you the coming months. Although at least it should start getting cooler."

"Thank goodness." Gabby managed a smile. "Do you think I could get an order of fries?"

"Sure thing, hon. I'll have those right out."

"Hungry?" Dane asked.

"No. Just needing to eat."

"Oh." What did that mean? Deciphering women had never been his strong point. He never lacked for dates, but also never seemed to get much past the initial stages. He'd been accused of spending too much time growing his law office. Now, spending too much time at the courthouse. He'd been told he was no fun. Apparently he lacked the *romance gene*.

"Have you—or your parents—heard from Ben lately?"

Stirring sugar into his coffee, Dane said, "He called Nana a couple weeks ago on her birthday."

"I was sorry to be out of town. She throws a good party."

He laughed.

Gabrielle was a certified massage therapist in a swanky local spa. But she also had a business degree, and put it to good use when she'd launched her own line of herbal massage oils. According to his mother, Gabrielle's schedule was filled weeks in advance. Proving that while her job might be touchy-feely, she had a good head on her shoulders. As such, Dane had always wondered what she'd seen in Ben—the perennial party boy. Aside from his humor and looks, he was a royal screwup. It took him six years to finish a four-year business degree. Got kicked out of his latest apartment for having forgotten to pay his rent. Oh—he'd had the money, he'd just been too busy to pay his bill.

Shaking his head, Dane sighed.

"What's wrong?" Gabby asked.

"Your boyfriend. My brother. What'd you ever see in him?"

"Well…" Had he imagined it? Or did her green eyes brighten just at the thought of Ben? "I suppose his sense of humor is what first attracted me to him. He's a great dancer. Mixes a mean margarita. Has a grin that never fails to flutter my insides. When he makes guacamole on Friday nights, he sings. He even—"

"You aware you're speaking of him in present tense?"

"Am I?" She sipped her juice, and it didn't escape his attention that her hands trembled. "That bother you?"

"No. I just…" What? What was his problem? Ben had already irrevocably hurt this woman. Why couldn't Dane at least allow her the comfort of reminiscing over happier times? "I guess I'm still so ticked off at him. You know, for what he's done, that—"

"It took two to tango, Dane. I could've said no to *doing the deed* without protection."

He blanched at her unexpected crudeness.

"Sometimes I get the feeling you hate your brother."

"I don't hate him, I just—"

"What? Intensely dislike him?" A sarcastic laugh escaped her. "No matter what you think of Ben, a part of me will always love him. He's the father of my child, and—"

"You don't think he's coming back to marry you, do you?" Fairy tales had never been Dane's preferred genre.

"No. Even if he did, I wouldn't take him back. He hurt me. Bad. So why are you hell-bent on hurting me again?"

Good question.

Lucky for Dane, Candace arrived with Gabrielle's fries.

"Thank you," Gabrielle said, reaching for the ketchup, then unscrewing the bottle's top and glopping the red stuff on her plate.

"You're welcome, hon. Anything else?"

"Do you have chocolate milk?"

"Sure do. Be right back with that, and a refill on your coffee." She nodded to Dane's empty cup.

"Chocolate milk probably isn't the best choice for you," Dane said.

"Acting as if you have the right to tell me anything about what's good or bad for me probably isn't the best choice for you." As she notched her chin higher, the light behind her eyes now seemed like a challenge.

"Point taken." When the waitress approached, he shoved his mug toward the edge of the table.

"I just took a cherry pie from the oven," she said to Gabrielle. "Want some with a scoop of vanilla?"

"Yes, please. Sounds delicious."

Once the chitchat-prone woman left, Dane reached

for the sugar packets. "Pie? I told Mama we'd be home for cake."

"Sugar?" she sassed, eyebrows raised over his using three packets. "Plus, *you* told your mother we'd be back for cake. Not me. I need to go home. I've had enough family time. The only reason I was even at their house was because your mom sounded so sad on the phone."

"How so?" he asked, sipping the steaming, fragrant brew.

"The way she went on about how worried she was."

"About what? Ben? The kid always manages to land on his feet."

"Not everything revolves around Ben's mistakes, Dane. Your mom confessed that she worries if Ben doesn't return home, I won't bring the baby to visit. She's really looking forward to becoming a grandmother, and Lord knows, she doesn't have much hope in you."

Ouch. He supposed he'd had it coming, but Gabrielle's verbal barb hit uncomfortably close. "How about we declare a truce and talk about what we came here specifically to discuss?"

"Fine with me," she said, dredging a fry through ketchup before shoving it in her mouth.

The waitress came and went with the pie, and damned if it didn't look good. Judging by the melting ice cream oozing over the generous slice, it was still warm from the oven. Dane had always had a sweet tooth. Usually, for his mother's and grandmother's baked goods, but in a pinch, anyone's baked goods would do. "Mind if I have a bite?"

She frowned. "You're kidding, right?"

Proving he wasn't, he snatched her fork and helped himself.

"Hey!" She grabbed her fork from his hand. "Get your own."

Dane grinned, then asked, "Getting down to business, when and where is this Lamaze thing?"

"I told you back at your parents' I'd rather use a friend."

"And I told you, I won't hear of it. This baby is my brother's responsibility. Since he's not here to handle the issue, I'll be his proxy."

Jerking a fresh napkin from the dispenser, Gabby used it to wipe her fork clean. "While you may view my baby as a responsibility, Dane, to me, he or she is my future child. So to hear you bloviating about responsibility and my pregnancy being an issue kinda makes me want to either puke or punch you. The verdict's still out on which way I'll eventually go." She forced a huge bite into her finally quiet mouth.

"Again, Gabrielle, I'm sorry. I've never really been the flowery type. I genuinely want to help you." *Not to mention keep his nagging mother off his back.* For most men, being told they were on the verge of becoming a father would be a time to rejoice. But for Ben, it'd just been one more chance to shirk adulthood. As for Gabrielle, though she was a fairly free-spirited sort, he'd thought she was too smart to have hooked up with Ben. "Think of it, you and me in one of those Lamaze classes filled with pregnant women. Has there ever been a clearer case of the proverbial odd couple?" Chuckling, he added, "Seriously, we'll probably share a lot of laughs."

"Or be laughed at," she said around her latest bite of

pie. "Why won't you just let me ask around the spa for a partner?"

"Maybe because a part of me wants to do this for you. Sure, ninety-nine percent of this mission is family duty, but you seem to be a good girl. You got a raw deal having Ben leave you."

"Really? You were sorry about Ben leaving? I never thought you even noticed I was alive."

"Don't sell yourself short. Our whole family gets a kick out of you." Would now be the time to confess the hip-hugging red dress she'd worn to his aunt Katie and uncle Paul's fiftieth-wedding-anniversary party still popped up in his dreams? Probably not, which was why he leaned in, saying, "Please, Gabrielle, do me the honor of allowing me to be your Lamaze coach. Not because my mom wants me to or because of any other family obligation I might feel, but because I'm guessing now— more than ever—you need a friend. Maybe Ben will be back in time for your big event—if so, great. If not, I don't want you to be alone. I want your baby to know Uncle Dane's got his or her back."

Tears swelled in her eyes.

His guess was that she was too stubborn to let them fall, but nonetheless, they were there. Evidence that finally, on a night where his foot had more often than not been in his mouth, he'd said the right thing.

"Thank you," she said, carefully pressing the tines of her fork to the pie crumbs. Though she didn't meet his gaze, he sensed relief emanating from her. Saw it in the relaxed set of her shoulders. The loosened hold on her fork. The way her lips had plumped back into their usual soft bow.

Swallowing hard, he looked to his coffee.

Yes, he would help Gabrielle through Lamaze and whatever other "husbandly" assistance she may need. But that's where it ended. She loved Ben, and for all his trash talk about his kid brother, Dane loved him very much, as well. The time for name-calling and pointing the finger of blame was long past. Now was the time for coming together as a family and making lemonade from lemons.

Dane had contacts whom he would pay generously for their help in tracking down Ben. After which, Dane would make him see what a precious gift he'd been given in having Gabrielle's love.

Chapter Two

"Breathe," Dane commanded.

"What do you think I'm doing?" Gabby fired back, in no mood for his commandeering ways. Though this was the first night of Lamaze, already their drill sergeant of an instructor was acting as if all twelve teams present would be giving labor any second. *"Hoo, hoo, hee, hee... Hoo, hoo, hee, hee..."*

"Are you supposed to look grumpy?" he asked, peering at her from where she awkwardly sat between his legs, her back snug against his chest. The pose felt distractingly intimate. She was having a hard time remembering a single thing that Regina, their instructor, had taught.

"Are you supposed to be getting into my business?"

"Just asking. I figure our instructor wouldn't want you scaring your baby with those furrowed brows."

"Bite me!" she muttered under her breath.

"Gabrielle and Dane?" Regina asked. "Is everything all right?"

"A-okay," Dane said.

Gabby jabbed him between his ribs.

"All right then, teams, for our next exercise…"

"Relax," Dane whispered in Gabby's right ear.

His warm breath raised goose bumps on her arms. Not exactly conducive to serenity. "Stop it."

"What?" he asked, all innocent.

"Trying to be nice after you've already been so mean."

"How have I been mean?" His latest whisper caused her to shiver.

"That crack about me scaring the baby wasn't very nice. And when your mother called my house to see if you'd found it all right, did you have to tell her I wasn't hungry for pot roast because I'd just finished a pizza?"

"No, but *did* you eat the whole pizza?"

Teeth clenched, she growled.

"I rest my case. Now, seriously, chill…" While she made a halfhearted attempt at following the breathing exercises, Dane kneaded her shoulders. Far from relaxing her, the all-too-pleasurable treat rocketed through her, consuming her with impossible-to-deal-with emotions. As a professional masseuse, it was a rare gift for her to be on the receiving end of a massage. Dane was Ben's brother. Obviously, any attraction for him wasn't real. What she was feeling was merely appreciation for his having soothed her aches.

Focusing on the here and now, on the very real issue of her impending labor, she tried blocking out her partner. True, easier said than done, but with any luck, he'd get squeamish during the birth videos and bail on his family honor. Then she'd return to plan B, which was using a friend from work as her coach.

Even worse than her choice of partners was a matter she dared not discuss with anyone. Not her friends. Never Dane. She just couldn't voice her concerns about the baby—it was like a nightmare you didn't want to talk about for fear of it coming true. Her ob-gyn told her everything was fine—both with her and the baby. But for the past few weeks, her inner voice said the doctor was wrong.

Despite the room's incandescent light, ultraplush white carpet and the soothing scent of lavender, she still struggled with a serious case of jitters. Not even the calming classical music wafting from discreet speakers helped. The mystery pain in her back was at least lessened by Dane's capable hands, but not completely gone.

"You've gone quiet," Dane whispered. "Everything all right?"

She nodded, then tossed in a rhythmic, *"Hoo, hoo, hee, hee,"* for good measure. But how *could* everything be all right? In thirteen painfully short weeks she would not only be going into labor *without* her baby's father, but she would be raising their child all on her own. Her conscience told her that with the help of good friends and Ben's family, she'd no doubt be fine, but the bigger her belly grew, so did her misgivings.

And what was up with the air-conditioning in this place? Didn't anyone know August in Arkansas was hot? Fanning herself, she asked, "How was I?"

"According to the chart," he said, nodding toward the breathing-technique chart their Lamaze instructor had placed on the overhead projector, "you need more emphasis on the *hees*."

"Way to inspire confidence, there, coach."

"Well, you asked."

"*Well*," she said in the most forceful whisper she could muster while lying in the infuriating man's arms, "you could've lied!"

"DON'T YOU EVER STOP EATING?" It wasn't so much Gabrielle's slit-eyed stare telling Dane he'd said the wrong thing, but the gaping mouth of the old busybody at the table across from them at Farelli's Pizza who'd been so engrossed in their conversation that she hadn't heard what her husband had said.

"Don't you ever stop nagging?" Biting into her fourth slice of sausage, mushroom and extra cheese, she closed her eyes and smiled.

At which point, Dane discreetly adjusted his fly and scowled. Damn, if her satisfied expression didn't resemble that of a woman enjoying a whole 'nother variety of fun.

"See that blonde over there?" she asked, shaking Parmesan cheese on her slice.

"Yeah. What about her?"

"Isn't she in our class?"

The pregnant, crazy-curly blonde in question waved, as did her equally blond and smiling coach. Dear Lord, twins? Identical save for the size of their bellies, they leaned in for a speedy discussion, then one grabbed their drinks, and the other snatched the remaining half of a pepperoni pizza.

"Hi," said the one sporting a belly bulge and dimples. "Hope you don't mind us barging in like this, but I noticed you're from our Lamaze class, and if we don't talk to someone else about it, we're going to burst!"

"Oh my gosh," Gabrielle said in an uncharacteristic teen-style gush, "I feel the same. Please, sit down. I'm Gabby Craig. He's my coach, Dane."

"You two married?" the nonpregnant twin inquired.

"No," Dane said, shifting to make room for the pair to sit.

"Then how'd you get to be a coach?" the pregnant twin asked.

"Long story," he said with a grunt, wishing his Coke were a beer.

"Oh." Having the good graces not to further press, the pregnant one extended her hand to Gabrielle. "I'm Stephanie Olmstead, and this is my sister, Lisa."

"Where's your husband?" Gabrielle asked.

Both blondes paled.

Lisa started to say something, but Stephanie cut her off. "M-Michael died. He is—was—a navy pilot stationed in the Middle East."

"I'm so sorry," Gabrielle said.

"It's okay," Stephanie said, reaching for a slice of their pizza. "I mean, obviously, it's not, okay I mean. But what're you going to do? Thank goodness for my sister, or I'd be a complete basket case instead of only half of one."

A round of laughter eased the tension Stephanie's confession had created.

"Excuse me…" The busybody from the next table glared. "Would you all mind holding it down. I can hardly hear *my* husband speak."

"Sorry." Gabrielle flashed the crone her first genuine smile of the night. "We'll keep it down."

Was it wrong for Dane to want that smile all for himself? After all, he was the one doing the work here. Chaperoning one pregnant woman was tough enough, but to now have two? What had he gotten himself into?

As if fate had been listening in on his internal lament, yet another pregnant woman strolled up with her coach in tow. "I don't mean to interrupt," said a redhead who somehow managed to pull off a black maternity power suit. She looked familiar. A fellow attorney he'd seen around the courthouse? He guessed so. "But we're also in the Lamaze class, and wouldn't mind hashing over a few points—that is, if you all don't mind?"

"Of course not," Gabrielle said, cramming Dane even farther to the edge of the oversize corner booth. "Welcome."

Introductions were made. The pregnant newcomer was Olivia Marshal. Her coach, Jen. The woman talked too fast for Dane to even catch her last name—not that it mattered. He didn't plan on making a habit of dining out with all these pregnant women after class.

"WELL?" MAMA BOCELLI ASKED Sunday afternoon, hovering behind Gabby with a steaming platter of chicken Parmesan. Her hair was piled high atop her head, crowned with a yellow scarf that matched her pleated yellow skirt and jacket. "How was your first class?"

Recalling the all-too-pleasurable feel of Dane's fingertips kneading her aching shoulders and back, Gabby had a tough time holding on to her composure.

"Um, class was fine," she managed to say, thanking Mama for the meaty-cheesy serving she'd placed on her plate.

"Just fine?" Nana asked. She also sported a crown of big hair, only hers was white with a red bow. "You didn't see any good, gory birth videos? My friend Stella said her granddaughter was thinking of launching a new video line called *Births Gone Wrong*."

"Nana!" Mama scolded. "What's gotten into you?"

"What'd I say?" she asked, all innocent while stealing a guzzle of Pops's wine. "The births turn out fine. The moms and babies all live. Only some of the babies have pointy heads—but even those eventually flatten out."

"Stop," Mama demanded, "or I'm sending you to your room."

"Even try it," Nana said, notching her chin, "and I'll run away! Edgar's got a new Chrysler 300, and I'm sure the backseat's plenty big enough for shacking up."

Mama slammed the platter onto the lace-covered table before making the sign of the cross on her chest.

After dinner, but before dessert, while Pops napped, Dane and his mother washed dishes and Nana gossiped on the phone, Gabby had been ordered into the living room to rest her feet. She'd tried explaining that she hadn't even been *on* her feet and would happily help with the dishes, but Mama wasn't having anything to do with it. Truly, Gabby guessed she just wanted her out of the way so that she could scold Nana in private, but with those two, who really knew?

Flipping through channels on Pops's new flat-screen

HDTV, she settled on a decorating show. They were finishing a nursery, which should've been fun to watch, but only reminded Gabby of how much work still needed to be done on her baby's room.

"Got indigestion?" Dane blurted, in his usual blunt, anything-but-suave manner, collapsing onto the brown leather recliner alongside hers.

"No. Why?" She frowned all the harder at the screen.

"You've got an awful look on your face."

"That's because she hasn't been able to figure out how to assemble the baby's crib." Mama sighed as she sank into the room's third recliner. One for every occupant of the house. Much to Mama's secret shame, Nana's recliner was custom purple suede.

"What's the matter with it?" Dane asked.

"Nothing," Gabby hastily said, regretting having ever mentioned it to Dane's mom. "I've got it handled. I'm sure one more read-through of the directions will yield phenomenal results."

Dane grunted. "Ordinarily, I'd love to help, but I've got an office football game this afternoon."

"Good. Because I've got it handled."

"If you could handle it," Nana said, wandering into the living room, holding her hand over the mouthpiece of the cordless phone, "then you would've already put the damned thing together."

"Nana!" Mama complained.

Nana stuck out her tongue.

SUNDAY NIGHT, FIERY ACID indigestion did little to help in Gabby's crib-assembly process. Yes, she probably needed someone's help, but certainly not Dane's! Besides, seeing how she was only a few months shy of being a single mom, it was high time she figured out how to do lots of things on her own—including carpentry.

Brave words, considering her baby's designer oak crib currently resembled storm-scattered tree limbs.

"Relax," she told herself, trying not to cry. "Follow the instructions and it'll be a piece of cake."

Around ten, she was thinking the task was cake, all right. Disgusting, dried-up Christmas fruitcake that'd been left in a box until Easter.

She trudged on until midnight, ignoring her aching back and feet and every part in between. Damn, Ben. He should be here for this kind of thing. In movies, wasn't the baby's daddy always there to rub feet and backs and put together bikes on Christmas Eve? Did Ben ever even feel guilty about what he'd done in leaving her pregnant and on her own?

When the crib was finally done, Gabby would've liked to have put on the sheets and bumper pads and hung the lamb mobile, but she was simply too tired. There was always tomorrow. At least tonight she'd proved that she wasn't completely helpless. Though it had taken her a while, she knew now she could handle it. Just like she would every other aspect of parenthood.

Sure, her conscience was only too thoughtful to point out, *you handled the practical part of getting ready for Baby, but how are you going to cope with loneliness? Having no one with whom to share Baby's first smile or coo?*

Ignoring her buttinski conscience, Gabby took a quick shower and put her aching body to bed.

Only trouble was, once she touched her head to her pillow, sleep didn't come, but thoughts of Ben, overlaid by contrasting images of his confounding brother, kept her awake for hours.

FOR THE THIRD TIME IN three weeks, finding himself seated among five women—three of whom were looking ready to burst—it occurred to Dane that he may need to get a life. At the local Cineplex, he sat in a much lower row than he usually preferred. Go figure, none of his *dates* could climb stairs. The lights had just gone down, meaning his two hours of sitting through a torturous chick flick were about to begin.

During a preview for an action thriller called *Thunder Kill,* he winced during a particularly loud explosion.

"You all right?" Gabrielle asked under her breath for only him to hear.

"Ah, sure," he said, searching her face in the dim light. "Why?"

"You seem quiet. This must be a drag, huh? Chaperoning all of these raging hormones?"

"It's not so bad," he said, regretfully admiring her glow—evident even in near darkness. She was taller than Stephanie, but shorter than the rest of their friends, and he thought Gabrielle was hot—in a pregnant kind of way. Call him crazy, but something about the contrast of her perfectly straight black hair combined with her out-of-control midsection bulge was infinitely appealing. He also liked her green eyes. Lighter than the fir tree in his parents' backyard, but darker than freshly mown grass. Gabrielle was a looker, and at the moment, those bewitching eyes of hers soothed him the way being outside on a sunny day always did.

"Good. I'm glad the night isn't a total bust."

"Not even close." A fact he'd only just realized.

"You said you have a lot of reading to do on your current case. Having us drag you along isn't going to set you back, is it?"

"Probably. But it's okay." With his thumb and fore-finger, he rubbed weary eyes. His job used to be every-thing to him, but lately, he didn't get the same high from being in court. A side effect of maturity? His sense of wanting more? A wife, a family to come home to instead of his empty house? How much of his anger with his brother had to do with the fact that Ben had had all of the above not once, but twice, only to throw it all away? What was it about Dane that made him want to commit, but he couldn't find the right woman? Ben, on the other hand, found all the women, but was incapable of committing.

"I'm worried about you," Gabrielle whispered. Had he been a weaker man, her warm breath in his ear might've been his undoing. "These past few weeks, you've seemed…" She cast him a faint smile.

"I know.…" He wanted to say more but couldn't. What was there to say?

"Dane?" Gabrielle's arm rested next to his on the armrest. Had he imagined it, or had she stroked his pinkie finger with hers? Swallowing hard, he clenched his jaw. For both of their sakes, he hoped she hadn't touched him. He didn't need that kind of pressure in his life. The kind that came from keeping his hands off his brother's girl.

"You going to eat those?" Stephanie reached across Gabrielle to snatch some Milk Duds from his box.

Trying not to scowl, he motioned for her to go ahead. Not that he'd needed to bother, seeing how she'd already crammed them into her mouth. For sanity's sake, he seriously needed to lay off the pregnant chicks and start hanging out more with the guys.

"Oh—Dane…" On his left, Olivia swallowed her latest bite of popcorn. "Steph was telling me how Gabby's having a tough time assembling Baby Günter's changing table. She's too proud to ask," she said with a cheesy grin in Gabrielle's direction, "but do you think you could help figure it out?"

What was it with Gabrielle refusing to ask for his help? Worse yet, why was a part of him secretly jazzed at the excuse to see her outside of class again?

"I'm doing fine in the assembly department," Gabrielle protested, casting a glare in her new friend's direction. She'd only just told Steph that she was having a baby boy and had probably assumed the news and subsequent baby-name discussion would be kept in confidence. "And no way am I naming my son Günter."

Olivia said, "Yeah, maybe nice, safe *George* would be best."

"I don't know," Dane interjected, helping himself to a Milk Dud before the pregnant ladies ate them all. "If the kid ever wants to make it big in Germany, Günter sounds perfect."

He laughed, dodging a few well-aimed pieces of popcorn.

"For that," Olivia said, "you *have* to help Gabby with her changing table."

"Why am I in trouble?" he teased. Flicking popcorn from his shoulder, he turned to her. "And for the record, I'd be happy to help with the changing table. As payment, I'll accept a couple dozen of your supposedly legendary cookies."

"Thanks," Gabrielle said, still glaring Olivia's way, "but I really don't need—"

His once jovial mood deflated by the fact that Gabrielle obviously didn't want him in her home, Dane barked—unfortunately during a preview of a quiet tearjerker, "Knock it off. If you need help, why didn't you just say so? I'll be over Saturday at one."

"REMEMBER, LADIES," REGINA SAID Thursday night, midway through their latest lesson, "*intense* labor pain is normal, but with properly controlled breathing, you should manage to ride out the increased severity of each contraction."

While Gabby worriedly cupped her belly, Olivia rolled her eyes.

The always calm and in-control lawyer whispered, "Controlled breathing, hell. The reason I signed up for this class was because I thought all of that huffing and puffing magically erased the pain. Now I'm thinking of going with Plan B—an e-epidural."

Stephanie snorted.

Dane shook his head.

Gabby, Lisa and Olivia's best friend, Jen, made gallant attempts to hide giggles.

"*Ladies!*" Regina glared their way. "This isn't fourth grade."

"I realize that," Olivia said, "but honestly, how much pain can mere breathing be expected to control?"

Their instructor took a few seconds to compose her thoughts—or maybe just to keep from strangling Olivia. From her angle across the dimly lit room, Gabby couldn't be sure which.

"Ms. Marshall…" Regina said, the tightness in her tone suggesting that Gabby's antistrangulation hypothesis was correct. "I think you're forgetting that present-day Lamaze concerns a great deal more than mere breathing. When you get a chance, please refresh yourself with the Lamaze Philosophy of Birth. But in the meantime, to answer your question, there are many ways to ease pain. Warm baths. Aromatherapy. Soothing music." The instructor smiled. "If you'd like more suggestions, feel free to talk with me after class."

"Ouch," Stephanie whispered once Regina continued on with the night's review of the stages and phases of labor. "Sign me up for the epidural, too."

While Olivia and Steph joked back and forth about how they planned to tackle labor, Gabby listened intently, soaking up each morsel of information. To say she was apprehensive about giving birth would be the understatement of the century. Petrified was more like it.

Her back still hurt. Mystery pains plagued her. No matter how much everyone from Mama Bocelli to her ob-gyn told her that her pregnancy was progressing fine, something just felt *off*.

One of the best things about this class was that for the blessed few hours she was surrounded by friends, she forgot to worry—at least about her health or future as a single mom. In class, her only problem was acting normal around Dane. The more she was around him, the more attractive he seemed to become. Something about him was a little untamed. A little wild. Exciting, even, from the standpoint that he always said exactly what was on his mind. She'd never been around anyone like that. Anyone so unafraid to say what needed to be said. At first, the quality had driven her nuts, but like the rest of him, it was growing on her.

"Psst…" Stephanie elbowed Gabby. "You up for Chinese food after class? I'll die if I don't have sweet-and-sour pork—stat."

"Mmm," Olivia interjected. "Cabbage egg rolls."

In her periphery vision, Gabby caught Dane's grin.

"I'M STUFFED," GABBY ANNOUNCED at Wong's—their favorite Chinese buffet. Pushing back her plate, she poured fresh hot green tea, wishing for one of her oversize mugs as opposed to the teeny, tiny china cup.

"You've hardly eaten a thing," Olivia said, snagging a fried crab wonton.

"Sure I did," Gabby lied. "This was my second plate."

"Nope," Stephanie said. "The second time you got up, all you took were a few slices of cantaloupe."

"Does it matter?" Gabby asked, forcing a bite of broccoli, wishing Dane's thigh wasn't brushing hers in the cramped booth. Was he staring? She felt hot, like he might be, but she didn't want to look.

"We're worried." Olivia covered Gabby's hand with hers.

"Really, guys, I'm fine." Aside from wishing the night would end! Something bugged her about being this close to Dane. Surely it was pregnancy hormones rocketing heat through her every nerve? "I must still be full from too much lunch."

"When are you starting your leave?" Olivia asked.

"In eleven weeks. I've got massages scheduled right up to my due date. And on the baby front, aside from assembling the changing table—which Dane is helping with on Saturday, I'm pretty much good to go."

Which was a good thing, right? So how come the knot in her stomach was still filled with dread?

After their meal, Dane—ever the gentleman—walked Gabby to her car. Her back was throbbing, and had she known him better, she would've liked holding on to him for support. As she stood next to her Jeep, her left hand pressed to the small of her back, she said, "Thanks for tonight. It was fun."

"My pleasure," he said with a genuine smile. "Bothering you?" he asked, nodding toward the area she favored.

"A little. It's no biggie."

Taking her keys, he opened her door for her.

"Probably normal, even, considering the size of my stomach."

Not looking convinced, he said, "You should get it checked. Can't be too careful."

"I will."

"Promise?"

Sighing, she rolled her eyes. "I'll be fine, *Dad*."

"Hey—I'm serious." As always. What if just once Dane loosened up? But still keeping the parts of himself that were more responsible than Ben. "You can never be too careful."

"Dane…" Knowing the impossibility of such a cosmic request, she tapped her left foot. "I don't mean to be rude—and I certainly appreciate the fact that you even care, but really, I'm good. Back pain is normal. All of my pregnancy books say so."

Too bad those same books failed to mention why every time Dane stood near, her pulse fluttered.

Chapter Three

"How did you get so good at carpentry?" In the baby's room, from her perch on the edge of a beruffled and pale blue daybed, Gabby swallowed hard. Dane had worn a tight T-shirt, and the breadth of his shoulders had her a little off balance. Or maybe it was his chiseled profile? Or the way his hair curled the slightest bit against the nape of his tanned neck? As he worked the shrieking power drill, his fingers were nimble. Strong and capable. A far cry from the disaster she'd been with the drill.

Dane laughed. "I'd hardly call this carpentry, seeing how all of the pieces came out of a box."

"As much as it pains me to admit, after having put the crib together, when it comes to furniture assembly, even the fast-food variety is over my head."

Shrugging, sitting back on his haunches, he said, "Back in my college days, I was king of ready-to-assemble. Bookcases, entertainment centers, dressers. If it was cheap, my apartment usually had it."

"Where did you go? To college, that is."

"Mizzou. How 'bout you?"

"University of Tulsa—second generation."

"Impressive," he said with a whistle. "Isn't that private and pricey?"

"Yes and yes, but I was on scholarship."

Nodding, he said, "You would be."

"What's that mean?"

"Nothing bad." He grunted while turning his latest screw.

"Then how come you had a tone?" Standing, hands on her hips, she added, "See if I bake any more cookies for you."

"Hey, whoa. Let's not get carried away. All I meant was that from the outside, you strike me as the classic overachiever type. Like anything you set your mind to comes easy—except for furniture assembly." He grinned.

She didn't.

"Anyway," he continued, "aside from falling for Ben, you seem to have a pretty good head on your shoulders."

Rolling her eyes, Gabby left for the kitchen, rubbing her aching lower back

Unfortunately, Dane followed.

On the kitchen counter sat dozens of cookies. Sugar. Snickerdoodle. Chocolate-laced oatmeal.

His size dwarfing her once-adequate kitchen, Dane rummaged in the cabinets for a glass, poured himself some milk and then helped himself to a seat on one of the three counter bar stools.

"Comfy?" she asked, arms folded, lips pressed together.

"Yes, ma'am. Thanks for asking." While she stood fuming, he downed three cookies, and then finished off his milk. "Ben was right. These are seriously good. Why aren't you a professional?"

She laughed. "Like a baker?"

"Yeah, why's that funny?"

"Only because in a way, with my massage oils, I kind of am—you know, like a specialized pastry chef. Mixing this and that to turn out just the right confection."

"Any plans of starting your own spa?"

"Maybe." She fought the urge to tell him to mind his own business. "Right now, my Internet sales are enough for me to live off, and all of the labor is subcontracted. Getting in touch with my clients, brightening their lives, is where my heart truly lies."

Eyebrows raised, he asked, "Getting *in touch?*"

"Ha, ha. For the record, I only have female clients— most of whom are middle-aged and overly stressed with the knotted muscles to prove it."

"Sorry," he said, and, to his credit, reddening. "I guess that stereotypical sexy masseuse image is tough to get out of my head."

"Why, Mr. Bocelli," she sassed with some sarcasm, "I wasn't aware that your big head had any room for thoughts of little old me."

After clearing his throat, he nodded toward the living area. "Moving on to a safer subject, this place is amazing."

"Thanks." For some odd reason, it warmed her to her toes that he enjoyed her eccentric decorating taste. Dane being Dane, she'd figured him for the type who'd look down on her mismatched home. "I'm addicted to antiques stores and flea markets. Yard sales, too. You just never know what you might find. Which I guess is why

I have a decorative representation from every era." Climbing onto the stool beside him, she added, "I'm particularly proud of my orange seventies sofa."

Laughing, Dane said, "It's actually in pretty decent shape, considering it's older than either of us."

Gabby smacked his shoulder.

"Hey," he complained, rubbing his wound, "that hurt."

"So did your dig at my furniture."

"Sorry. I was teasing. It's incredible how you pulled all of this together. Kind of like you made a home for everyone's leftover junk. Only it's not junk anymore, because you made it nice."

"Thanks," she said, wrinkling her nose. "I think."

Tucked between comfy brown leather armchairs was a fifties side table crowned with a Tiffany lamp. Fawn-toned walls provided the perfect backdrop for Gabby's heirloom needlepoint collection, as well as oil-painted landscapes. Leafy ferns and bamboo palms brightened corners. Set at an angle was a rattan chaise fitted with a downy cushion that made it perfect for lazy after-noons spent reading.

"What are all of these?" he asked, gesturing to her most prized collection of trinkets she'd grouped on a glass-topped sofa table. The tiny boxes were shaped in everything from pea pods and carrots to the Taj Mahal.

"Limoges. They're hand-painted from France."

"Cute. How long have you been collecting?"

"Years. They're all over the house." Crossing to a glass-fronted china cabinet, she pulled out a tiny pink VW Bug. "This was my first. My parents gave it to me—along with the real deal—for my college graduation."

"They gave you a pink car?"

"Red car," she said with a reminiscent grin, thinking back to that special day. "My dad used to decorate it for Christmas. He made a giant goofy hat from felt."

"You don't have it anymore? To put on your Jeep?"

"No." Putting her box back in the cabinet so Dane wouldn't see the tears forming in her eyes, she said, "Now that Mom and Dad are gone—and Ben—I have a tough time with Christmas."

"I'm sorry," he said, his tone softer than it'd ever been before.

"When my parents were alive, Mom always made a big deal out of the holidays. I've got all of her decorations. I'm thinking that for the baby's first Christmas I'll start our own traditions. We'll make it a big deal." Forcing good cheer, she asked, "Want to come?"

"Sure. I love a good party."

You do?

Seeing how, to the best of her knowledge, always-dependable Dane avoided partying like the plague, she took his statement as a stab at a joke. Ben was the family good-time boy. Everyone loved being around him. He was one of those people who instantly lit up a room. Just being around him had been magical. Kind of like Christmas—but in human form.

After an awkward silence, Dane cleared his throat. "This should be a special year for you, what with the baby and all."

"Uh-huh." Drawing her lower lip into her mouth, Gabby nibbled at it tensely.

"You don't look especially excited."

"I am," she said, heading for the kitchen pass-through counter where she'd set the cookie platter. Taking one, she bit a peanut butter ball rather than her lip. "Just scared. Tired. Overwhelmed. Wondering if I'm being foolish in thinking I can handle it all, but not really having much choice."

"Fair enough." After more silence broken only by a copper fountain's trickle, he asked, "If the subject is off limits, and feel free telling me to butt out, but what happened between you and Ben? I mean, other than him just taking off? I thought you two were solid?"

Wow. Where to start? For that matter, considering who she was seated alongside, did she even want to start? Oddly enough, even though she was still livid with Ben, a part of her was still loyal to him. Especially knowing how Dane seemed to take every opportunity to slam his brother down.

"Um… Long story short? He found out I was pregnant and freaked. About two weeks in, the night I'd expected him to propose, he announced he was sorry, but wasn't ready to be a father. Too many wild oats left to sow."

"*Jackass…*" Dane mumbled under his breath.

"I shouldn't have even told you," she said in Ben's defense. "Why do you hate him so much?"

"I don't hate him. For crying out loud, he's my brother, but what's wrong with you? What kind of hold does he have on you that here you are, about to pop with his baby, you haven't so much as heard from him in months, yet you're still jumping to his defense?"

"I'm sorry. He *is* the father of my child. Shouldn't I owe him some loyalty for that?"

Dane snorted. "If you were an adoring poodle. Aren't you the least bit angry for what he's done?"

"Duh. But what good is getting mad going to do? I don't even know where he is. How can I rail on him?"

"But you would? If you could?"

What a loaded question. Would she? Really, let Ben have it?

Sometimes, yes.

Sometimes, no.

Obviously, if she'd loved Ben enough to make a baby with him, her feelings ran deep. Yes, she wanted him to, along with her, take responsibility for the child they'd be bringing into the world, but who wanted to force a guy to marry you? It was kind of like having Mama Bocelli approach Dane about helping out with Lamaze coaching—humiliating. Granted, Dane, with his over-blown sense of family pride, most likely would've stepped in regardless of what his mom wanted him to do, but that was beside the point.

Gabby had her own inborn sense of pride, and it would've been nice if at least one of the Bocelli men had wanted to be with her out of love. Or, in Dane's case, friendship rather than duty.

Still, considering what a monster of a time she'd had assembling the crib, and how badly her back had been hurting, it was a wonderful feeling knowing she wasn't completely on her own. Even if he had been coerced into it, Gabby was profoundly grateful for Dane's help.

WHILE GABRIELLE CONTINUED to bake, Dane finished the changing table. He couldn't say what had gotten into him to have gone off on her. Maybe since the first time Ben had sung her praises, Dane had been secretly resentful. Why would such a seemingly perfect woman even want Ben?

For that matter, why did he even care?

He suspected it had something to do Naomi, who'd once claimed to love Dane. Right. Which must be why she'd dumped him for Ben after meeting his brother at a Sunday family dinner. Dane had been so certain about Naomi having been *the one*.

He'd wanted to marry her.

Start a family with her.

Which was yet another reason helping Gabrielle was fulfilling yet maddening. The fact that in a perfect world, he'd be assembling furniture for his own son or daughter. Instead of getting easier, being around Gabrielle and her bulging Lamaze buddies was growing harder by the day. The closer they came to giving birth, the more he wanted a kid of his own.

"Looks good." Leaning against the open door, Gabrielle nodded toward the changing table.

"Thanks," he said, gathering his tools. "Your latest batch of cookies smell great."

Shrugging off his compliment, she said, "Sorry you got roped into helping me yet again. I'm sure you've got better things to do."

Shrugging, he said, "There's still plenty of time left in the day."

"Yeah, but…."

He glanced her way, only to get a shock. Her color wasn't just *off,* but lurking somewhere between the shade of a café latte and Pepto-Bismol. Abandoning his gear, he rose. "Is your back bothering you?"

"No." Clenching her jaw and pressing her hand to her lower back, she turned to leave the room.

"Not so fast," he said, lightly grasping her upper arm, wishing her pained expression didn't oddly slice through him. "Has this been going on awhile?"

"No. Not long."

Stealing a moment to ponder the statement, he asked, "Yeah, but wasn't your back hurting the night of our last Lamaze class?"

"No," she lied, tugging free from his hold. "I probably just need a nap. That's all."

"Uh-huh. Where are your shoes?" he asked, eyeing her fuzzy, tie-dyed slippers.

"For Saturday afternoon, I'm wearing them, see?" She gave a sassy foot wiggle.

"Gabrielle," he said, noting the forced lightness of her tone, "this is no joke. You're, like, a year pregnant. As a favor to me, please, let's run you to the E.R. We'll be back before you can say Baby Günter."

"That's right," she quipped, tottering down the hall. "Because I'm not going any—" Wincing so hard tears escaped the corners of her eyes, she clutched the wall.

"That's it...." In about two seconds, he'd scooped her into his arms. "Where's your purse?"

"Put me down," she protested. "If, after my nap, I'm still hurting, I'll get Steph or Olivia, or even your mother, to take me to the doctor."

"Trust me, if you call Mom, Nana will want to come, and then the two of them will make you feel even worse."

She couldn't help but laugh at his joke—especially seeing how it was probably true.

"Like it or not," Dane said, "you're going with me." Assuming the oversize designer bag on the counter to be her purse, he snatched it on his way out the door.

"Put me down," she ordered along with a wriggle that made it tough to keep a strong hold on her and search for her keys. "This is ridiculous. I'm—"

"Holy crap, Gabrielle, quit fighting me and hush. Whatever's going on with you, I *felt* it. It's like your whole body tensed."

Forehead beaded with sweat, she nodded, resting her cheek against his shoulder. "It probably wouldn't be a bad idea to get this checked out."

"You think?" he said with a strangled laugh. Eyeing a front porch swing, he gingerly set her there while he fished through her monstrosity of a purse. Her key ring featured a stuffed, red-sequined heart. When he clutched it, an obnoxious electronic version of "That's Amore" filled the sweltering early-September air.

"I-isn't that cute? Ben found it for me in Eureka Springs."

"Swell." Door locked, his own keys in hand, Dane navigated the jungle of hanging and potted ferns, flowers and gnomes, to find his way back to her. "Your insurance card in your wallet?"

Eyes closed, biting her lower lip, she nodded. "B-but if you'd just call Olivia, she knows all of my vitals. We exchanged info—j-just in case."

Ignoring her latest protest was easier than hefting her

back into his arms. Even though she was only twenty-nine weeks into her pregnancy, she looked ready to pop.

"I can walk," she complained.

"I'm sure you can," he said, footfalls heavy on the porch's whitewashed, wood-plank floor. Lord, but it was a scorcher outside. "How're you doing?"

"G-great," she said, teeth chattering as he headed down a winding stone path to her driveway, temporarily setting her to her feet while opening the passenger door of his black Escalade. Chattering teeth? On a blazing-hot, pushing-triple-digits day? Not a good sign. "I just need a good nap."

"Right." With the door open, his aching back wasn't too happy about hefting Gabrielle onto the passenger seat, but the task was soon enough finished. Once he'd buckled her in and, since she had no lap, set her purse on her slippers, he shut her door and circled to his own side of the car.

Behind the wheel, he asked, "You okay?"

"I-I'm good. Feeling m-much better." Her sideways panicked grin told a different story.

Revving the engine to life, he peeled out of her drive, aiming the powerful vehicle probably way faster than he should've down the quiet, maple-lined street.

With Gabrielle's each breathy moan, panic seized him.

"Is my baby going to be okay?" she asked, voice faint, as if drifting through a fog.

"Damned straight," he said through gritted teeth, zigzagging around traffic on the more heavily used main artery.

"C-can you please f-find Olivia? And Steph?"

"Sure," he said, wanting to hold her hand but, considering the vehicle's current speed, needing both of his on the wheel.

"Promise? It r-really hurts, and I'm—"

He was on the verge of telling her anything to ease the worried frown between her brows, when she slumped over in her seat.

"Gabrielle?" Checking her out, he fishtailed.

The guy behind him honked, then flipped him off.

"Gabrielle!"

With the hospital a mere block away, he pushed the vehicle's speed to well over the legal limit.

Tires squealing, he rammed the car to a stop beneath the E.R.'s covered portico.

Leaping out, and nearly strangling himself on his still-fastened seat belt, he left the car running while bolting for the E.R. entrance.

Out of breath, but full of determination, he stormed to the front of a three-patient-deep line.

"Sir!" the scrub-wearing clerk shouted above already hostile protests. "You'll have to wait your turn!"

"Sorry," he said, "but my—" What was Gabrielle to him? Not his wife or girl or mother of his child. An acquaintance, really.

"Your what, sir?"

"My, um, friend…" Dane finally decided upon. What was wrong with him? His chest tightened. Was he having a freakin' heart attack? "I'm afraid she's losing her baby."

Chapter Four

"Did you ever find Olivia and Steph?" Gabby asked, squeezing Dane's hand as he walked beside the gurney toward the elevator leading to the hospital's fifth-floor labor-and-delivery unit. A brief examination had determined her to be seven centimeters dilated, but her water hadn't broken. After having read nearly a dozen pregnancy books, how could she have been so foolish as to not recognize signs of early labor? "I'm not ready. This can't be happening."

"It'll be all right," he said, smoothing stray hair from her forehead when her nurse stopped the gurney and pressed the up button. "I'll find them."

"Your mother and Nana? I changed my mind, and do want to see them."

"Absolutely," he assured her. "I'll find anyone you'd like. But I'm sure this will turn out to be no big deal."

Though she nodded, the searing pain that was now not only in her back, but abdomen made her doubt his words. Was her baby in danger? Throughout her pregnancy, she'd worried about an event just like this. Had she done something wrong? Not paid close enough attention to her diet? Pushed herself too hard at her biweekly expectant mothers' yoga class?

With a ding, the elevator doors swished open.

The gurney's jostle over the threshold worsened her pain. To keep from crying out, Gabby bit her lower lip. The overhead fluorescent lights were mercilessly bright, so she closed her eyes on them. On the reality they forced her to face. Behind closed eyes, her baby was fine and so was she. The screaming pain was gone and she was back home, her son in her arms, seated in the cozy new rocker she'd only recently had delivered.

"We're almost there," the nurse said when the elevator jolted to a stop.

"Sir, as the baby's father, you'll need to stop at the desk to fill out a few forms."

"I'm not—"

"He's not—"

"Dr. Pool!" the nurse called, ignoring them both.

A woman Gabby had never met jogged their way. "Mrs. Craig?" she asked with a warm but concerned smile.

"It's *Ms.*," Gabby said. "I'm going to be a, ah, single mom."

"Oh." After a glance Dane's way, the doctor made a notation on her chart. She asked him, "Are you a family member?"

"Yes," he said. "And Lamaze partner."

"Okay, then," the doctor said, dizzying Gabby when she directed the nurse to circle back, rolling her in the opposite direction. "Ms. Craig, let's get you to a room."

"Dane, it hurts," Gabby said through a fresh on-slaught of pain. "I don't want to be alone."

"I won't leave you," he assured her, grasping her hand.

"Thank you." She managed a faint smile before the nurse wheeled her into a private room.

When Dane tried following, the nurse cut him off at the pass. "If you'd wait outside, we'll get Ms. Craig changed."

AFTER REASSURING Gabrielle that he wouldn't go far, Dane abided by the nurse's wishes and now walked blindly down the antiseptic-smelling hall, barely dodging a food cart and two robe-wearing patients strolling with IV poles. Away from the bustling nurses' station and crowded waiting area, Dane found a windowed alcove occupied by two shabby blue chairs and a side table piled with fingered magazines and a potted ivy. Stumbling into a seat, he hunched over, resting his forearms on his knees.

Why did this feel so personal? If something hap-pened to Gabrielle or her baby, the loss would be incon-ceivable. But she was Ben's girl. The baby, Ben's. Not only was it dishonorable for Dane to feel any connec-tion beyond friendship for Gabrielle, but self-destruc-tive. Neither she nor her baby would *ever* be his.

So why was his heart pounding? Why were his mouth dry and his palms wet? Why? Because the God's honest truth was that his time with Gabrielle had turned into much more than the cleanup job he'd expected. Being with her was no longer solely about making good on his little brother's mistakes, but trying to put meaning into Dane's own life.

Only since spending time with Gabrielle instead of

focusing on his career had Dane realized just how much he had left to figure out. Namely, how to get through the remainder of Gabrielle's pregnancy without losing his mind.

"IS IT NORMAL TO HURT THIS BAD?" Gabby asked the nurse once she'd changed into her hospital-issued gown.

"'Fraid so," the older woman said, patting Gabby's blanketed thigh. "And I hate to tell you, but if the doctor can't stop your labor, it's going to get worse before it gets better."

Gabby groaned.

Hands cupping her bulging belly, she squeezed her eyes shut and prayed. For her baby. For her friends and the Bocellis to soon be with her. For her to have the strength to see this through.

"Sir?" Across the room, the nurse who'd introduced herself as Nancy held open the door. "You're welcome to come back in."

Dane, decked out in blue scrubs and paper booties, entered while Nancy left. "You decent?"

"Sort of," Gabby said, flopping her hands at her nonexistent waist.

"What'd I miss?" Snagging a guest chair, he moved it closer to the head of her bed. With sunlight streaming through generous picture windows and the room's yellow-and-white-striped wallpaper, floral bedspread and matching drapes, Gabby could've almost imagined herself at a hotel—almost. The steady, reassuring beep of the fetal monitor gave away the illusion. As did the too-tight blood pressure cuff and IV making her left arm throb.

"How're you doing?" Dane asked. "Need anything?"

Wincing through another contraction, she shook her head. "Thanks, though. Did you have any luck finding my friends?"

"No, but I left messages with everyone."

Nodding, Gabby said, "Thanks."

"You bet." Covering her hand with his, he asked, "I saw the doctor come in. What'd she say?"

"To try and stop my labor, they gave me a steroid shot. But at twenty-nine weeks, if my labor can't be stopped, the doctor said my baby will most likely survive, but could suffer all kinds of things like respiratory distress, sleep apnea, eye problems and even sudden infant death syndrome, so…" Her eyes stung with tears, but she didn't want to cry. She wanted to stay positive. Correction—she *would* stay positive.

"The key thing to remember is that your baby could have any one of those problems, or *none*. So see? Sounds to me like either way the night goes, you and your little guy are going to be great." He smiled, and if only for that instant, she believed him. Yes, her labor would be stopped and her baby would be fine. A couple of months from now, her baby in her arms, she and Dane would laugh over this close call. She and Dane. It was nuts how much she'd come to depend on him in such a short time. Or was it just emotional spillover from Ben causing her to lean on his older brother?

"Thirsty?" He offered her a spoonful of ice chips, which she gladly accepted, relishing the cool moisture in her parched mouth. "Thanks."

Nodding, he asked, "Need anything else?"

Wincing through her latest contraction, she said, "Distract me."

"How am I supposed to do that?"

"I don't know," she grumbled through the most intense part of the pain. "Think of something. Tell me a story. What were you like in college? Were you always the polar opposite of—arrrrgh—B-Ben? Or did you used to be different?"

The question caught Dane off guard.

Especially since the truth—the exact, biting moment he'd changed—had been forever burned into his memory. But since he wasn't a masochist, the incident wasn't often revisited.

"Please…I've got to have something to get my mind off this pain."

"Okay, well…" A story, huh? Clearing his throat, he said, "Point of fact, my brother and I have more in common—or, at least, we used to—than you might think. In college, I had a knack for throwing the best *gatherings* on campus. I got roped into being my frat house's party chair."

"Like theme stuff? Or just regular booze—arrrrgh—fests?"

He chuckled. "Both of the above, but to back up a little—not to mention defend myself—I do come by my appreciation for a good time honestly. You may not have noticed," he said in a teasing tone, "but my crazy Italian family looks for any excuse to celebrate." Chuckling, he added, "I swear, if I so much as brought home an A on a math test—Ben, a C—Mom would bust out the good china and call the grandparents over for a feast."

"Sounds a-amazing," Gabrielle said. Was there a wistful note to her tone?

"It was." Back then, though Ben had still been a screwup, they'd at least been friends.

"You're l-lucky. My cousin, Kate, and her family are all I have left. But they live in northern Kansas, so I don't see them much."

He couldn't fathom not being surrounded by family—even though his was sometimes a pain. "How long ago was it?" he asked, stroking sweat-dampened hair from her forehead. "Since you lost your folks?"

"Six years. Th-they were rafting the Colorado River. It was supposed to have been the vacation of a lifetime. A storm hit miles upstream. Caused the box canyon they were in to flood. Their raft capsized, and— Arrrgh!"

"I can guess the rest," he said, tightening his hold on her clammy hand.

When Gabrielle's next contraction hit, Dane swore he felt it with her. She held on to him for all she was worth, and he returned the favor.

A knock sounded at the door, and in walked a huge bouquet of baby-blue carnations and baby-themed Mylar balloons. "Hello?" Stephanie called out. "Anyone home?"

"You came." Gabrielle held out her arms to her friend. "I'm so glad. Thank you."

"Wouldn't have missed it," she said. "But I couldn't find Olivia. Her cell's off. I think she's out for an early dinner."

Gabrielle managed to laugh through a grimace. "I'm glad someone's having fun."

"Now that I'm here," Stephanie said, sending a grin Dane's way, "you'll have fun, too. I'm only too happy to rescue you from Mr. Personality."

"He's—arrrgh—actually been a godsend. I didn't want to be alone."

"I know the feeling." Expression wistful, Stephanie twined her fingers through the curling ribbons dangling from the balloons. "It's good we found each other."

AT A LITTLE AFTER 2:00 A.M., Gabby woke, momentarily disoriented.

Save for the light spilling through the open bathroom door and the glow from the various monitors, the room was dark. The fetal monitor showed her baby's heartbeat to still be regular and strong.

"How do you feel?" Dane asked, his voice coming from the shadowy corner. He stood, then walked into her view, resting his hand atop hers. "You've been sleeping for hours."

"Where's Stephanie?" Gabby's mouth was dry. Her lips felt cracked. Every inch of her body ached as if she'd spent the afternoon hauling bricks.

"I sent her home at midnight. She looked beat. The whole family was here, but once your contractions slowed, and then stopped, Mom and Pops took Nana home to bed."

"Then I'm okay? The baby?"

"Perfect," he said, lacing his fingers with hers. "Your nurse told us the doctor will be by in the morning to sign your release papers."

"That's it? Just like that? What caused me to go

into early labor?" She tried sitting up, but it took too much effort.

"The nurse wouldn't tell us a damned thing, other than that for the moment you and Baby Günter are fine."

"Why'd you stay?" she asked.

"I promised I wouldn't leave you alone, remember?" His smile radiated strength. Assurance. Comfort. "We're partners, right? In this together?"

"How come you never showed this side of yourself while Ben and I were together?"

He pulled his armchair to the head of her bed and sat. "What *side?* With me, what you see is what you get. Maybe you just haven't been looking."

She laughed. "I suppose that's one way of putting it. Seriously, Dane, when I was with Ben you were stand-offish to the point of being rude. What was up with that? Because the more I'm with you, the more I'm seeing a side of you I never knew existed."

Arms crossed, he leaned his head back. "Any particular reason you're choosing now to bring this up?"

"There's nothing better to talk about. I mean, I'd like to drill my doctor, but seeing how she won't be here for at least five or six hours, I might as well drill you."

"Thanks." Stretching, he eased his legs out in front of him, crossing them at the ankles.

"Seriously, Dane. I'm curious."

"As well as a pain in my you-know-what." Sighing, he cast her a wary gaze. "I stayed away from you because I figured any woman with Ben had to have a loose screw."

She rolled her eyes. "There's the Dane I know and love."

"Love, huh?" He winked.

Had she had a spare pillow, she'd have pitched it smack between his infuriating eyes. "You know what I mean."

"Yes, I do, and in case you haven't noticed, I'd just as soon talk about something else."

"Why?"

Sighing, he said, "Because the topic is asinine. I'm the same man I've always been. Will always be. The only thing that's changed is you. Before now, Ben has been the focus of your attention. You're thinking, Where is he? When is he coming home? Why did he leave? Was it something I did? Said? If I could replay our last time together, would it make a difference?"

"Stop," she said in a sharp whisper. Dane's words pricked her already tender emotions. "I don't think any of that," she lied. "You act as if I have nothing better to do but pine after your brother like some lovesick teen."

"I'm sorry," he said, easing upright. "Calm down before you bring on a fresh batch of contractions."

"Like you'd care?" She instantly regretted her harsh words. Of course he cared, or he wouldn't be there. The question was, why did he care?

"How LONG?" GABBY DIDN'T MEAN to come across as dense to her doctor, but surely she'd heard wrong. No way did she have time to be on total bed rest until the end of her pregnancy. "I misunderstood."

Making notes on Gabby's chart, Dr. Yan, a petite brunette, grimaced. "Sorry, but yes, I did say you're out of commission until this baby's ready to be safely out of your oven." Chart closed, the grinning doctor patted

Gabby's belly. "Before I sign your release papers, I need to know you have round-the-clock care."

"Done." During the doctor's visit, Dane stood, arms crossed in the corner, leaning against the wall. "I'll make all the necessary arrangements."

"Dane," Gabby objected, "you've already done too much."

"This isn't the time to be prideful," the doctor said to Gabby. "You need help. Now, from all of the tests we've run, there's no reason you shouldn't be able to carry this baby to term—*if* you stay off your feet."

"Why is this happening?" Gabby asked. "Have I done something wrong?"

"Not at all," the doctor reassured her. "I wish I had a definitive answer for you, but for all we know about the human body, sometimes Mother Nature does what she wants."

Hating the tears stinging her eyes, Gabby wrapped her arms protectively over her stomach. Damn Ben. If only he'd stayed, maybe her stress level wouldn't have been quite so high. Moreover, she wouldn't be forced to accept Dane's charity—again.

After the doctor had left final instructions, a nurse removed Gabby's IV and monitor connections before helping her dress in a red maternity warm-up suit that Stephanie had brought by. Waiting for an orderly to come with a wheelchair, Gabby couldn't remember a time when she'd felt more helpless.

"Quit scowling," Dane said.

"I'm not," Gabby protested. "Why would you even say such a thing?"

"Because you are. This is the same frowny face you had when I forced you into going to the E.R. The face that says, *I'm letting you help me, but only because I have no other option.*"

Though Dane had captured her mood with uncanny accuracy, she'd never admit it. "Leave me alone. I don't even like you."

"Aw, now," he said, his tone signaling he was on the verge of giving her grief, "how can you say that when just last night you were telling me how much you love me?"

"What is this? National Pick on Pregnant Women Day?"

"You didn't get the memo?" Damn him, but his broad smile made her stomach flip-flop. What was wrong with her? Other than the obvious baby-health issues, was her subconscious developing a *thing* for Dane? If so, it needed to stop!

Chapter Five

"This'll do," Dane said after checking out Gabrielle's guest room. It was a little flowery for his taste, with wallpaper that looked like daisies had been thrown at it, but he'd bring over a flat-screen TV and his laptop along with a few other electronic gadgets and he'd be right at home.

"What?" Gabrielle called out from her room.

"Nothing! Just talking to myself." They'd only been back at her place for ten minutes, and already she'd been a handful. Complaining about him carrying her to her bed, whining about him putting too many blankets over her, demanding he stop bringing her food when the doctor specifically said she'd need regular meals.

"When you get a chance, could you please come here!"

He stopped in the doorway of her room. "What's up?"

"I've been mulling over this whole bed rest thing, and I'm thinking the doctor must've misdiagnosed my condition."

Perching on the foot of Gabrielle's bed, he asked, "Have you already forgotten the miracle you've been granted? This time yesterday, we were afraid you were losing your baby. Now all you have to do to keep him safe is stay put. Why is that so hard for you?"

"I-it's not," she said, her gaze darting anywhere but at him. "This has all happened so fast, I'm not sure what to do with myself. Nancy, the spa owner, was great about contacting all of my clients, and my accountant already handles most of my Internet sales. But I hate feeling like I've just dumped my responsibilities on friends."

"Why does that sound like only a portion of the truth?" He patted her quilt-covered leg. "Talk to me. Tell me what else is eating you."

For the longest time, she said nothing. Her lips moved slightly, as if she wanted to speak but couldn't find the words. Finally, in a halting tone, she said, "Have you ever stopped to consider that my added problem might be you?"

"Me?" He laughed. When his cell phone rang, he said, "Hold that ridiculous thought."

While his secretary confirmed potential court dates, Dane tried focusing, but even though he'd wandered into the living room, he couldn't get Gabrielle's words from his head. By the time Cassidy had finished scheduling the upcoming week, he rushed her through closing pleasantries, fighting a flash of guilt for not wanting to hear about her toddler's latest amazing feat.

A good ten minutes later, the call finally done, Dane returned to Gabrielle only to find her sleeping.

Damn. What had she meant? How could he be the root of her problems when he'd done nothing but turn his entire life upside down to accommodate her?

WAKING AFTER A NAP, Gabby felt bad for going off on Dane the way she had, but she didn't regret it. Part of her resented his presence in her home. Another part would be forever grateful. Her problem was figuring out how to unite her warring halves.

At least if she had to be stuck someplace for the next couple months, her room was pretty. She looked around, admiring the pink-and-white wallpaper with a lacy floral border that matched her vintage, wedding-ring-patterned quilt designed with a white background and plenty of gold-and-pink-toned calico squares. Her vanity table and dresser were mahogany, purchased at auction for far more than she should've paid, but she loved them. A plush gold velvet fainting couch occupied a windowed alcove, along with potted ferns and a tall palm. Pink gingham crowned with antique lace covered her matching night-stands. Crystal lamps, her favorite books and plenty of silver-framed photos of her parents and friends topped both tables. A comfy, oversize floral armchair occupied the wall next to her bed. Antique botanical prints in ornate gold frames decorated the walls. She loved this room. She'd be fine being cooped up in here if it weren't for…

"Feel better?" Dane leaned against her bedroom door, a sandwich in his right hand. "You were seriously out of it."

"It's unnerving."

"What?" he asked around a big bite.

"The thought of you watching me while I'm sleeping."

"It wasn't like that," he said. "I checked on you. Your eyes were closed. End of story."

Hearing him say it like that—so matter-of-fact—made

her feel stupid. Like she was making a big deal out of nothing. But was it really nothing when just being near him made her pulse race as if she'd been jogging for an hour?

"Earlier," he said after finishing his last bite, "when you said I was your problem, mind telling me what you meant?"

Suppressing a groan, Gabby rolled her eyes. "I was just in a bad mood, all right? You have to admit that this whole situation is weird. I mean, you pretty much moved yourself in. You didn't even ask."

"Sorry," he said, looking more bored than apologetic, "but it's not like you have a lot of options."

"Thanks for reminding me," she snapped. Though she had Dane and his family, her new Lamaze buddies and a few friends from work, Gabby never had felt more alone. Her only real family was Kate, yet she lived too far away to be of any practical help. "Did it ever occur to you that this is hard for me? Being your charity case?"

Rolling his eyes, he said, "That's ridiculous. You're pregnant with my nephew. That makes you family. I'm just sorry that I wasn't there for you earlier."

His caring brought an instant knot to her throat. Swallowing, she managed to say, "None of this is your fault. Your responsibility."

"I get that." Tone gentle, he added, "But what's it hurt if I view this situation as a practice run? You know, trying to juggle a successful career and a happy home? You want the truth? That's something I've never been able to do." Sitting on the foot of her bed, he stared out her bedroom window. "No matter how hard I try, I'm all work."

"That's not true," she said, wishing she were allowed

to sit up. To comfort him with a hug the way he'd soothed her with words. "Look how much time you've spent with me lately. Assembling the changing table. Never leaving my side at the hospital. You've been amazing. I don't even know why I said what I did. Pregnancy hormones, I guess. They make me cranky."

As for what his nearness was doing, the heat radiating from him, she didn't know how to compartmentalize the emotions it swelled within her. There was too much all at once.

"Let me help with that, too," he said, stroking her feet through her blanket in what she was sure was supposed to have been a comforting manner, but felt jarringly erotic. "What can I do to help make you un-cranky? Need ice cream? Gummie bears? Are pickles still popular with the mother-to-be crowd?"

Grinning, she shook her head and said, "You're lucky I'm stuck in this bed, or that comment would earn you a pillow beating."

"Sounds hot," he teased, infuriating her all the more. "But seriously, anything you need done as far as getting ready for the baby? Tell me. I'll make it happen."

"Thank you." She wanted to meet his gaze but couldn't. Something about this man she hardly knew offering her the words she'd so desperately craved hearing from his brother were her undoing. Tears stung her eyes. Hoping Dane wouldn't see, she swiped them away.

"What's wrong?" Too late, he'd not only seen her tears, but edged farther up the bed. Instead of stroking her feet, his big hand now rested atop Gabby's belly.

Heat licked through her, warring with her already heightened senses.

What was wrong? he'd asked. Try everything! It was against every notion of common decency for her to be turned on by Ben's brother. But, in her hormone-addled mind, maybe Dane was merely a stand-in for the man she wanted him to be.

Ha! Her conscience railed. With each passing day, out of the two Bocelli brothers, Dane was proving to be the only true man.

"LOOK WHAT I BROUGHT ESPECIALLY for you," Mama Bocelli said to Gabby the next morning. Dane had long since left for the courthouse, assigning Gabby's care to his mom. Mama set a breakfast tray across Gabby's lap, and then a silver-framed picture of a smiling Ben on her bedside table. The ham-and-cheese omelet paired with homemade croissants and fresh fruit salad had looked and smelled amazing. However, upon seeing Ben's face—even in photo form—Gabby's stomach roiled. "My boy's such a handsome thing," the older woman said, angling the frame just right before flicking at an invisible speck of dust marring the glass. "He'll be back, you know. Mark my words. He'll return just in the nick of time to share in your baby's birth."

"Mama," Gabby said, not even sure where to start. "I can't thank you enough for this delicious meal, but the photo—of Ben— I know you meant well, but…"

"Pooh," Mama said, leaving the room for a minute and returning with a glass of orange juice. "I know how much he hurt you, sweetheart, but even you must know

he cares. That he'll eventually cure himself of his wan-
derlust, and—"

"Please," Gabby urged, "just leave it alone. I'm fine
without Ben. Dane is—"

"Dane is a dear boy for coddling his mother's wishes,
but ultimately, he's not your baby's father."

"You think I don't know that? Besides which, Dane
is hardly a boy. He's a fully grown man who…" What?
*Has cared for me more in the past month than Ben did
in the year we'd dated?*

"I'm sorry," Mama said uncharacteristically—apolo-
gizing for her wrongdoings had never been a strong
point. "Vincent is all the time telling me to mind my
own business. But when you were last over for dinner,
I couldn't help but notice the sadness in your eyes."
Patting Gabby's hand in the Bocelli way, she said, "I
want to help. *Please* let me help."

How was Gabby supposed to reply? On the one hand,
she'd never needed assistance more in her life. On the
other, constantly being reminded of the mistake she'd
made in ever having fallen for a guy like Ben couldn't
be healthy—for her or her unborn child.

"Of course I'd love for you to help," Gabby said,
trying to keep her tone gracious instead of impatient.
"It's just that it's hard, you know. Going from being
independent to being waited on hand and foot. I'm not
used to it." *I miss my privacy. Nursing my emotional
wounds on my own terms. Not having Dane hovering.
Making me crazy with his intense gaze.*

"Sweetheart," Mama said with a cluck. "Before you
know it, our baby boy will be here and your roles will

be reversed. You will be constantly caring for him. What harm is there in taking this sliver of time for yourself? Let the people who love you pamper you. Really, it's okay. Ask me, you've always tried doing too much on your own."

And there you had it. The world according to Mama Bocelli. If only letting go were as simple as the older woman made it seem.

"I TOTALLY GET WHERE YOU'RE coming from," Stephanie said the next day at lunch, eating a messy duplicate of the meatball sub she'd brought Gabby. Next to the armchair, Mama Bocelli had set up a side table to accommodate visitors and an army of friends and neighbors who had worked out a food-delivery schedule. While it warmed Gabby through and through to be the recipient of such good will, she hadn't entirely adjusted to the situation. "Having some guy just move in would be tough, but I can think of worse things." Stephanie's latest bite cascaded marinara sauce atop her bulging belly. Lucky for her, in anticipation of making a mess, she'd piled napkins over the area most likely to be dribbled upon. "Especially considering how criminally hot the man is."

"Stop," Gabby pleaded, hoping her blush was only on the inside. "Dane's not exactly hard on the eyes, but—"

"Oh, no. You're not honestly going to sit there, denying you and the judge share a certain chemistry, are you?"

"We do not!" Gabby shrieked. "I got knocked up by his brother. All he feels for me is a sense of family duty. As for what I feel for him?" The spicy marinara sauce bubbled up her throat. "It's complicated."

"Uh-huh." Grinning, Stephanie nodded. "I'll give you that. Don't think Olivia and I didn't notice the way the man hovered over you at the hospital. To anyone who didn't know the truth of your situation, they'd think Dane was your baby's father."

BORED OUT OF HER GOURD, having watched an all-day marathon of a fashion-design reality competition that she'd already seen the first time the show had aired, Gabby was drifting off for her tenth nap when a key jostling the front-door lock jolted her awake.

"Hello?" Dane called.

Anticipation made Gabby feel like a wriggling happy puppy. "I'm in the backyard," she called. "You know, just mowing and trimming a few trees."

"Uh-huh," he said, casting her a lethally potent smile. He carried two bags. One, glossy black paper—the kind with handles and a decorative fluff of hot-pink tissue paper that looked as if it was from an exclusive boutique. The other was flimsy plastic, bulging with colorful items she could see but not identify. "You set one pretty foot near a tree, and I'll chop it off."

"Ouch." She smirked. "Are caretakers supposed to threaten violence?"

"When they have poorly behaved patients such as yourself—yes. Now, which present do you want first?"

"You shouldn't have brought me anything." Though she felt obligated to protest his actions, she secretly couldn't wait to see what was in the bags.

"Seeing how poorly you treat me, you're right. But

since I braved hellacious traffic on the off chance of making you smile, pick what you want to open."

"Thank you," she said. Having always been a firm believer in saving the best for last, she pointed to the less elaborate of the two bags. "I'll take that."

Handing it to her, he said, "I asked around the court-house what kinds of things most women enjoyed doing during their last few weeks of pregnancy, and this hobby won. Plus, I noticed how you have a thing for cook-ies...." He shrugged. His expression was one she hadn't seen before. Expectation? Worry over whether or not she'd like his gift? The Dane she'd once known wouldn't have cared.

Pulling out a cross-stitch kit, she beamed. "I've been meaning to get one of these, but never had the time. I tried it once, but the result was a disaster."

"I remember." Setting the fancier bag on the chair beside her bed, he shoved his hands in his suit pants pockets. "One Sunday, you and Ben showed up for a family dinner. You had a bandage on your right index finger. My brother said it was from you pricking yourself with a tapestry needle."

"H-how did you..." Surprise at his observation stopped her from finishing the sentence. She remem-bered, too. The way Dane hadn't said more than two words to her throughout the entire meal. Then he'd excused himself before dessert, claiming he had to study up for his next day's case.

Tapping his temple, he smiled. "I've always had a knack for remembering the little things."

"That's probably part of what makes you a great

judge," she said, smoothing her hands along the cool outer wrap of his gift. The picture was of a Blue-Willow-patterned cookie jar set upon a lacy cloth-covered table. Saucers of chocolate chip, oatmeal and what looked to be lemon bar cookies surrounded the jar. A crystal vase brimming with old-fashioned red roses provided just the right pop of color. Included in the kit were plenty of color-coded embroidery floss and several tapestry needles. "Really, Dane, I, well, this means a lot. It was incredibly thoughtful. Thank you."

"You're welcome." His oddly formal head bow made her think he felt embarrassed by the praise. "Want your other gift?" He wagged the shiny black bag.

"Yes, please." Removing the tissue revealed a sumptuous pair of bubble-gum-pink satin maternity pj's. She couldn't imagine where he'd found them. "These are… How?" Grinning up at him, she shook her head. "Dane Bocelli, you are some piece of work."

"Like them?"

"*Love* them. Come here." She held out her arms.

"What?" His furrowed forehead told her the last thing he wanted to do was meet her for a hug.

Ramming his hands in his pockets, he said, "Thanks, but I, ah, wouldn't want to hurt you."

"Hurt me? That's silly." What hurt was the fact that he apparently didn't want to touch her.

He shrugged. "What do you want for dinner? Mama was going to bring us something, but I told her you were on some special diet."

"Why'd you tell her that?"

Turning his back to her, he said, "Well, you know I

love my family, but I didn't want Mama and Nana and Pops over here all night. I've got briefs to read and laundry to do and—"

"Know what really sounds good?" Gabby said, still miffed by his slight but completely on board with his decision to indulge in a Mama-free night.

"What?" Expression wary, he glanced over his shoulder.

"Relax," she said with a forced smile, trying to forgive him. "In light of how much work you have to do, and how I can think of nothing more pleasant than changing into my new pj's and starting my cross-stitch project, I was only going to suggest you make use of the Chinese delivery menu conveniently located in the kitchen junk drawer."

"Need help changing?"

"Oh—you think I'm too fragile for a hug, but now, you're only too willing help me off with my clothes?"

He ducked his gaze. "I didn't mean it like that...."

"I know. I'm kidding."

Judging by his glare, he hadn't gotten the joke.

Chapter Six

IN THE KITCHEN, DANE RELEASED the breath he'd been holding for what felt like the past twenty minutes. He went through the motions of ordering dinner. From their post-Lamaze outings, he already knew Gabrielle's favorites. Once that task was completed, he headed to the guest bedroom where he'd set up a temporary office.

He booted up his laptop, took the files he needed from his briefcase, then he sat and stared at the screen.

"Gabrielle?" he called over the techno theme songs of one of her reality shows.

"Yes?" she shouted in return.

"Need anything?"

"No, thank you."

Damn. Why, he couldn't say, but the woman had become a welcome distraction. Shopping for her had been the most fun he'd had in months. Seeing her smile upon opening her gifts—better than Christmas morning.

As for her wanting a hug?

Torture. She'd no doubt meant it as a friendly thank-you gesture. Which, ordinarily, would've been no big deal. But something about her had been different. Her mussed hair and makeup-free complexion had caught him off guard. Somehow, seeing her in her usual neat and tidy garb made her unapproachable. This new look was infinitely more appealing. Invoking crazy urges to pull her onto his lap and do nothing all night but cuddle and eat Chinese food and watch movies. If a few kisses accidentally happened, so much the better.

Conking his forehead with his palm, hoping for clarity, he only grew more confused. Caring for her was supposed to have been no big deal. He hadn't expected mental flashes of her to pop into his head while court had been in session. He hadn't thought shopping for her would be more satisfying than reading the *Law Review*.

"Dane?" she called.

"Yeah?" he said, already on his feet, hating the rush of excitement that stemmed from just hearing her call his name. "What's up?"

"You're probably going to think this sounds goofy," she said, squinting while threading her embroidery needle, "but—"

"Try me."

Her shy smile lit his world. "I'm lonely. I know you have to work, but would you mind bringing your laptop in here?"

ALL THE NEXT AFTERNOON, Dane worked diligently to stay focused while in court, but on recess, thoughts of Gabrielle consumed him. What was she doing at that very moment? Which of her friends had stopped by with lunch?

Somewhere along the line, hanging out with her had stopped being a chore and started being a pleasure. He liked thinking about what to prepare her for dinner, and what they might talk about during their meal.

By the time he'd finished at the courthouse, and then hit the grocery store to pick up Gabrielle's favorite herbal tea, it was pushing six.

"Dane? That you?" Gabrielle called from the bedroom.

"None other," he answered.

"Come see me! I'm bored!"

On the way to her room, he ditched his briefcase, undid his top shirt button and loosened his tie. He smiled when he saw her. "Woman, you're a mess. You look like you're ready to be on some weird parade float a bunch of kids decorated with their mothers' embroidery floss."

The contents of the craft kit he'd purchased for her littered the bed and the enormous mound created by her bulging stomach. Her long hair was half up in a ponytail; the rest tumbled every which way about her shoulders and cheeks and forehead. Top all of that with her pink satin pj's and glowing complexion, and he'd never seen her look prettier. Like a rumpled fairy princess.

"Did I really ask you to come in here?" Her Highness sassed. "After that derogatory observation, you can turn right back around."

"Aw, I'm sorry," he said, planting a chaste kiss to the crown of her head. "I meant it all in good fun. Now, how about a change of scenery?"

"What do you mean?"

"How about I carry you into the living room, so that we can talk while I make dinner?"

"I can walk, you know." She graced him with the pout he now recognized as the first sign of her displeasure. The pout he could deal with. It was when she full-on frowned he knew he was in real trouble.

"Yes, I do know. I also remember your obstetrician telling you the only time you're to be on your feet is for trips to the bathroom and brief showers."

She had no comeback for that.

"Now, want me to carry you to the living room, or are you good in here?"

"Carry me, please." She plucked all of the scattered yarns from her chest and stomach, setting them atop her embroidery hoop before placing the lopsided pile on the nightstand—right alongside the grinning picture of Ben that his mother had so thoughtfully provided. She held out her arms, like an excited little girl, wriggling her fingers.

OVER THE NEXT WEEK, Gabby and Dane settled into a comfortable routine. If Dane cooked, he carried her to the sofa, allowing them to talk while he prepared their meal. Some nights, he picked up a homemade dinner from his mom or simply ordered delivery. In all cases, they ate picnic-style on Gabby's bed, watching movies, taking turns deciding what to watch.

Tuesday night after eating, as usual, Dane retired to the armchair at the head of her bed with a pile of legal-size folders on his lap.

Over the melodic rise of music in the tear-jerker chick flick Gabby had selected, he asked, "Tell me your interpretation of this."

Pausing the movie, she said, "Shoot."

He explained briefly that he needed her opinion on the closing argument from a child custody case he was to make a judgment on in the morning. Upon finishing the sad story about why a mother hadn't been able to properly care for her children, he asked, "What's your take?"

"Seeing how I haven't heard the other side—"

"I don't want you to. I just need your gut-level reaction to what I've just read."

Taking a deep breath, she said, "While what the woman has been through is a nightmare, her attorney has done a brilliant job of candy-coating fairly ugly truths. I'm no expert, but the fact that she *tried* rehab isn't the same thing as finishing, and then living a life without recreational drugs and booze."

"My thoughts exactly." He jotted a few notes on the margin of a document, then closed the folder, leaned his head back and shut his eyes.

"Does it ever bother you?" she asked, angling toward him. "The whole notion of literally holding people's lives in your hands?"

"Of course," he said, cracking open his eyes to peer her way. "But for the most part, it's not me making decisions, but hundreds of years of case law. Besides which, by the time plaintiffs appear in my court, there's a reason. We're not talking about folks randomly pulled off the street who have their children taken away. For every action, there's a legal consequence. Period."

"I get that…." She fan-folded the edge of her bedsheet. "I guess what I'm asking is, does it personally bother you being the one responsible for enforcing that law? You know, delivering the bad news."

Eyes fully open, he rubbed his hands along his whisker-stubbled jawline. "Guess I've never really viewed it that way. For as long as I can remember, injustice has pissed me off. Be it some kid in my class who got away with lying about why his homework wasn't turned in on time, or my brother pulling one of his stunts without a shred of repercussion, well…" He shrugged. "What can I say? Yes, it's sad when people screw up, but they made their own mess. I'm only trying to clean it up."

"I-is that what I am to you?" she quietly asked, not daring to meet his intense gaze. "Ben's mess you're *cleaning?*"

"Aw, Gabrielle…" Covering his face with his hands, he said, "We've been over and over this. I'll admit, when I first agreed to do the whole Lamaze thing, it did have a familiar feel. Like the times I'd have to do Ben's chores because he'd forgotten. But now that I've gotten to know you…" His words hung in the still air.

She looked up, momentarily startled when their gazes locked. Mouth dry, pulse oddly picking up speed, Gabby found herself not wanting him to finish his sentence. What if he admitted to thinking of her in terms of a friendly obligation? Although if he did, why would she care? She was resigned to the fact that for her baby to be born healthy, she'd have to swallow her pride and accept all the help she could get. But from Dane, she somehow wanted more. She didn't want to be an item tagged on to his already lengthy to-do list.

Clearing his throat, he set the folders that were on his lap to the floor, and then leaned toward her, grasping her hand. With his index finger, he lightly stroked the top of her hand. The simple motion shimmered through her with unbearable heat and light. "Now that I've gotten to know you, I—" an odd laugh escaped him "—I find myself looking forward to coming home to see you each night. I see why Ben was attracted to you, Gabrielle. What I can't for the life of me understand is how he so willingly let you go."

His admission was so startling, his voice so hoarse with emotion, Gabby was momentarily stunned.

"Please don't think that was some kind of pickup line, or that I'm coming on to you," he said quickly. "I'm just saying I enjoy your company, and I-I hope that you enjoy mine." He released her hand and then stood. "It's late. You should be getting to bed."

I've been in bed all day, Gabby wanted to scream. "We haven't finished the movie."

"It's a five-day rental," he said. "We'll finish up tomorrow." He leaned over and kissed the top of her head in a brotherly way. "Need anything before I lock up and hit the sack?"

"No, thank you," she said, trying not to cry. What she needed was for Dane to see her as a woman. But then, was that really such a hot idea? She'd already been devastated by one Bocelli brother. What was up with this insane craving to get mixed up with another?

ALONE IN GABRIELLE'S GUEST room, his door safely shut behind him, Dane slowly exhaled. Making light of his accidental admission had been tough.

Dane had never claimed to be anywhere near perfect, but one thing he wouldn't do was take his brother's girl.

That had been more Ben's style, and Dane swore he'd never be that kind of man.

What kind are you?

Were Dane's actions in caring for Gabrielle purely altruistic? Or, somewhere deep inside, was it about showing up Ben? Making Gabrielle want him over Ben.

Enough.

Above all, Dane prided himself on his keen sense of right and wrong, and no matter how much he was growing attached to Gabrielle, thinking of her in terms of anything more than friendship would be wrong.

THURSDAY NIGHT, AFTER THEY'D eaten one of Dane's surprisingly tasty hamburger-cheesy-noodle concoctions, he asked, "How do you keep all of that straight?"

"What do you mean?" Gabby fished through the bed linens for the precious last strands of #743 magenta. Her needlework was going along nicely, but she had a problem when it came to losing embroidery floss and the occasional needle. Sure, craft-type needles weren't all that sharp, but that didn't make them hurt any less when she rolled over on them in the middle of the night!

"I mean," he said from the comfy armchair at the head of her bed, "that night after night, I sit here, watching you lose all of your stuff. You need a system."

Rolling her eyes before threading her needle, she said, "You need to mind your own business. My current *system* works just fine."

"Whatever," he said with a put-upon sigh, turning his attention back to the night's Katharine Hepburn classic.

"You don't have to get snippy," she noted. "And, anyway, why do you even care?"

"I don't. I was just making conversation. And for the record, seeing how I've turned my entire life upside down for you, everything you do has somehow become my business."

"Okay, whoa." Setting her project atop her belly, she asked, "Are you saying you resent having to spend all of this time with me? Because—"

"Stop putting words in my mouth. That's not at all what I meant." Tone soft, a faint smile tugging the corners of his mouth, he said, "We're talking about your abysmal needlework habits. I've even found threads stuck to the bottoms of your socks in the dirty clothes hamper. What happens when you run out of colors before you finish?"

Squeezing her eyes shut, she wished him to be gone when she reopened them. No such luck. "Why are you so mean?"

"How am I mean for pointing out the obvious?"

"You're exasperating," she said, not wanting to think of him handling her intimate laundry. Not that socks were—intimate, that is, but still...Gabby had been under the impression that Dane's mother had been taking care of her laundry. "Don't you have anything better to do than harass a defenseless pregnant woman?"

"AND THEN HE ACTUALLY HAD the nerve to complain that I'm not neat enough while working on my cross-stitch. Can you imagine?" Further emphasizing her outrage, Gabby folded her arms.

Olivia politely covered a yawn.

"Sorry I'm boring you," Gabby snapped. "His demeanor is seriously annoying."

"Mmm-hmm." Grinning, Olivia gathered the remains of the fast-food salads she'd brought for Friday's lunch. "Are you aware that the only thing you've talked about for the past forty minutes is Dane? How *maddening* he is, and *annoying,* and *infuriating,* and—"

"Okay, I get the hint." Gabby reached for her embroidery hoop, catching a glimpse of Ben's picture on the bedside table. "It's just that I've been forced to be with Dane so much that he's all I can think about."

"Uh-huh." Olivia crossed her arms and smiled.

"What?"

"I think you know *what,*" her supposed friend said with a mischievous twinkle in her eyes. "You've got a crush on your baby's daddy's big brother."

"No way!" Gabby protested, hating the heat that flamed her cheeks. "Haven't you heard a word I've said about how awful he is?"

"The guy is pretty much your own personal hunk of a manservant and you're complaining?"

"It's not that I'm complaining, per se, just that—"

"If you didn't find fault with him, he'd be a little too perfect—unlike that loser brother of his?"

"Ben's not a loser," Gabby argued. "He's just going through a rough patch. You know, like trying to find himself."

"How can you lie there defending the creep? You're carrying his child, and he abandoned you. His amazing brother is picking up the pieces of your life. Dane is the

man you owe your allegiance to. If you're having
trouble seeing that, you've got a lot bigger problems
than being stuck at home on bed rest."

"I READ AN INTERESTING ARTICLE today," Dane said Friday
night. They'd just finished off a pizza, and as there was
nothing good on TV, and he'd forgotten to run by the
movie rental store, they had each immersed themselves
in their own activities. While Gabrielle read the book
she'd been working on for the past few days, he'd been
going over case law—and hating every minute of it.

"Oh?" She glanced up. "What was it about?"

"A golden mummy mask owned by an Egyptian
noblewoman was found in a storeroom at a St. Louis
museum. Apparently, it's been there since the fifties, and
is pretty spectacular. Now the Egyptian government
wants it back."

Resting her book face-open on her stomach, she
asked, "Did the article say how the museum acquired
the piece?"

"That's where the problem lies. The museum isn't
sure. Meanwhile, the Egyptians have detailed documen-
tation of where the mask was discovered and cataloged."

"Fascinating," she said, eyes alight with an inner
glow. "Stuff like that is so much fun to think about. Like
Indiana Jones, only in real life. So was the mask stolen?
Was it inadvertently slipped into a wrong shipment? Is
it part of a larger mystery? You know, like a long-
forgotten clue to some hidden global scandal?"

Her passion for the subject raised color in her cheeks,
making her infinitely more attractive. It didn't matter that

her ponytail was crooked and messy. He didn't care that she'd dribbled something red from her lunch down the front of her blue-and-white flannel pj's. All that mattered was that for the moment, she was healthy and happy and giving him the best Friday night he'd had in years.

"Dane? You okay?"

"Sure," he said, darting his gaze. "Just tired."

"You don't look tired, but deep in thought. What's up? Plotting an adventure for us once this little guy finally arrives?" Grinning, she patted her belly.

Lips pressed tight, if only for a second, he indulged in the luxury of how a life shared with Gabrielle might be. Long talks and laughter and travel anywhere in the world her heart desired. "Did you and Ben talk about stuff like that? Taking off on a moment's notice to some exotic locale?"

Nose wrinkled, she asked, "That was random. Why do you care?"

He shrugged. "No biggie. Just curious."

In reality, he'd asked because it ate him alive, imagining Ben doing anything with Gabrielle. But most especially he hated knowing Ben had shared hundreds of intimate moments like this, only to throw them away. Had Gabrielle been Dane's, he'd have treasured her.

"For the record," she said, her expression taking on a wistful air, "no. Ben's a lot of fun, but when it comes to anything remotely academic or deep, he checks out. Not that ancient mummy masks are a particularly deep subject, but you know what I mean."

Boy, did he. "Being in some sense a small-business owner, you're in a black-and-white world. How did you cope with Ben's…how should I put this? Um, penchant for *color?*"

"When he was here, it never even occurred to me how ill-suited we really were. But now, with you…" She ducked her gaze. "Well, let's just say you've opened my eyes to the fact that there's a lot more important things to look for in a grown-up relationship than round-the-clock fun."

Chapter Seven

Saturday afternoon, upon waking from a nap, Gabby was still mulling over a confusing mix of emotions. On the one hand, her conversation last night with Dane had been such a pleasure. They'd connected on an intellectual level in a way she and Ben never had. On the other hand, Gabby was stewing over Olivia's blunt statement. The one about her owing her allegiance to Dane. She had a habit of cutting straight to the heart of any given matter, making Olivia much better suited for Dane than she was. Their razor-sharp legal minds would be great together. They could just ride off into the sunset, making one big happy legal family. Meanwhile, here she'd sit, alone in her bed for all of eternity.

Jealous of Olivia being more Dane's type?

Her heart's question only made her more confused. Yes, she was jealous! But not because she wanted him in a romantic sense. Did she?

Maybe she was being overly hard on both Dane and Olivia, but she couldn't help it. Being two *years* pregnant and stuck on your back day after day tended to make a girl a little unreasonable!

And where was Dane? Last Saturday, they'd had a Scrabble marathon. The hateful creep had beaten her ten games to four. Still, the ones she'd won had been slaughters.

"Dane!" she called out.

No answer.

Her stomach growled. He'd promised grilled cheese and tomato soup for lunch. His mother had been scheduled for lunch, but switched to dinner because of a mix-up on her weekly hair appointment.

Sighing, Gabby switched off the cooking show she'd been watching. The Mexican fiesta casserole Chef Carole was preparing only made her more hungry.

Without watching TV, she didn't feel like working on her embroidery, so she set that to the bedside table, carefully avoiding Ben's smiling face.

She opened the romance novel she was three-quarters of the way through, but a few pages in, the hero and heroine shared a heated argument that resulted in an even hotter kiss. Frowning, Gabby marked her page, then set the book on her bedside pile—which was now thankfully tall enough that she couldn't see Ben.

"Dane!" she called again.

Still no answer.

Which only made her feel worse. How had she grown so dependent on him? Not just in the physical sense, but to the point that she missed his company? She'd always enjoyed Ben's company, but she also had never minded times when he hadn't been around. He was always *on,* which had compelled her to match his level of intensity.

Tossing back the covers, she struggled to her feet and waddled to the bathroom. Her center of balance was no longer centered!

At the sink, washing her hands, she found a note from Dane taped to the mirror. Since she'd been asleep, he'd left to run a few errands.

Knowing for certain he wasn't home made the house strangely quiet. Lonely. Once her son was born, at least she wouldn't be completely on her own, but she'd still miss Dane's presence when he returned to his own home. In her current frame of mind, the thought was too depressing to ponder.

Tottering back to bed, she pulled up the covers and promptly fell asleep.

"HEY, THERE, SLEEPING BEAUTY."

Gabby slowly woke, only to wonder if she was dreaming. Dane stood alongside her, his hand stroking her hair.

"Time to wake up. You've been sleeping all day."

"Since you abandoned me," she said, trying not to pout, "it wasn't as if I had anything better to do." Like stare at the way his navy T-shirt hugged his chest.

"Aw, now, don't be mad. I'm touched that you missed me, but I was only gone a few hours. Plus, my absence was for a good cause."

"Where were you?"

"Working on a surprise for you." He sat in the armchair next to her bed. He sighed. "It's been a long time since I worked with my hands. It felt good, but tiring in a different way from my usual."

"Huh? Tell me where you've been. All that handwork sounds a little kinky." Plus, as long as he kept talking, maybe she'd be able to focus on his words rather than his handsome, square-jawed face. Or the way he smelled faintly of sweet pipe tobacco and cedar.

"Get your mind out of the gutter. I've been at a friend of my father's wood shop. Making something for you."

"You've already done too much."

"True," he said, a smile warming his expression. "But I have to confess that the gift I'm about to present is partially for my own sanity."

"What's that supposed to mean?"

"Close your eyes," he directed.

Abiding by his request heightened her senses, making her even more aware of his presence. She knew when he'd left the room, but she most especially knew when he'd returned. Her entire body hummed.

"Okay," he said, "now look."

She opened her eyes only to wrinkle her nose in confusion. The woodwork was gorgeous, but she wasn't sure what it was. Part lap tray, part painter's palette, only with dozens of ring-size holes. There were slots along each side and maybe a cup holder—but again, she couldn't be sure. The smooth, dark cherry wood glowed with high-sheen varnish. Regardless of the item's purpose, a lot of heart and thought had gone into its creation. Throat tight, wondering how long he'd been sneaking out to work on the piece, she said, "Dane, it's amazing, but—"

"Lord, woman, can't you tell what it is?" Snatching a handful of the embroidery floss scattered across her quilt, he took back her gift before having a seat in the comfy chair next to her bed. After he'd had the mystery object for a few seconds, she understood—which only made the item all the more dear.

"It's an organizer," she said, pushing up in the bed. "And all of the little holes are for my floss."

"Ding, ding, ding," he teased. "You win. Or, maybe I win, since I won't have to look at your mess."

"You're awful," she said, holding out her hands. "Let me do it. I want to load it with all of my stuff." The slots were for everything from the TV remote to her craft pattern and embroidery hoop. And the hole she'd guessed to be a cup holder was exactly that.

"Sure," he said, handing it over. "But after you didn't even know what it was, I'm not sure you deserve the fruits of my labor."

"You're probably right, but I really do appreciate it." Temporarily setting the gift aside, she held out her arms for a hug. "Come here so I can thank you properly."

His normally handsome expression turned stricken. "Um, I'm good."

"Don't be ridiculous. Come here. I want to give you a hug."

He stood and begrudgingly leaned over her so that they could share an awkward series of pats. Disappointment made her eyes sting with tears, although she wasn't sure why. What had she been hoping for? Disney animals parading out of the closet in song? The man was Ben's brother. The only reason he was with her was his own honor. He wanted to make right all of Ben's wrongs.

From the foot of her bed, Dane gestured toward the kitchen. "Mom gave me a frozen casserole. I'm going to stick it in the oven for an early dinner. Need anything?"

Yes! her body screamed. But what she craved went far beyond his self-assigned duties. "No, thank you."

"All right, then. See you in a bit." And just like that, he was gone. His leaving felt as if someone had turned out the light on her mood.

IN THE KITCHEN, DANE BRACED his hands against the counter, kicking himself for even thinking about wanting what he could never have.

Refusing to waste one more minute feeling sorry for himself over the fact that Gabrielle had been with Ben first, Dane charged into action, shoving their meal into the oven before making a simple salad. He washed the few dishes in the sink.

He'd just set up camp on the living room sofa, settling in for a long night of studying transcripts and notes, when Gabrielle shouted, "Dane!"

His heart skipped a beat. She sounded horrible. Was she having trouble with the baby? Tossing aside his work, he ran to her. "What's wrong?"

"Nothing." She sat pretty as you please, grinning from ear to ear, displaying her now-filled lap box with all the panache of a game-show model. "Look, everything fits."

"You called me in here for that?" Hand over his still-pounding heart, he scowled. "You nearly gave me a heart attack."

"I thought you would be happy, seeing how you were the one all the time pointing out my mess." Removing the tray from her lap, she set it on the empty side of the bed. Arms folded, she said, "Never mind. I should've known this new-and-improved Dane was too good to be true."

"Oh, give me a break." Shaking his head, he said, "I'm going to blame that irrational statement on raging hormones."

"What else am I supposed to think?" she asked. "You won't even give me a decent hug."

"A hug? After all I've done for you, you're bitching about the way I hug?" He turned to leave the room. Women. They were all nuts. No wonder he'd been out of the dating pool for a while. To preserve his sanity!

"Come back here!" Her voice wobbled, and Dane thought he heard her sniff. Oh hell, she wasn't crying, was she?

"What?" he asked from a safe distance.

"Don't you *what* me. Dane, you've been amazing, doing so much, but…I know this must sound silly to you, but the thing I miss most about Ben being gone is simple physical contact."

Sighing, he said, "A hug, I can give you, but, Gabrielle, I've gotta put this on the table…if you're wanting more from me—like for me to take Ben's place in your life, I—"

"Of course that's not what I want," she said, sharply looking away. "And I resent you even implying such a thing."

"Good." Shoving his hands into his pockets, he said, "Now that we've got that settled, I'll finish dinner."

Is it settled?

In the kitchen's quiet, the question thundered through Dane's head. Slowly exhaling, he ignored his conscience's answer.

Not, no. But, hell no.

Living with Gabrielle had only made her more fascinating. Everything about her from her silly pouts to her intelligent conversations to her sexy-wild hair just intrigued him more.

"Dane!"

Groaning, he put the heels of his hands over his eyes.

"I'm sorry, okay? Please, don't be mad."

Edging toward her room, he said, "Honey, I'm not angry, just frustrated. I'm giving you everything I've got, but apparently that's not enough."

"Of course it is. I'm just more touchy-feely than you, and a good hug means a lot."

"Mmm-hmm." Hands back in his pockets, he dared ask, "What constitutes a *good* hug?"

"You know, like generate some warmth. Hold someone long enough to know they've been held."

Rubbing his aching eyes with his thumb and forefinger, he said, "Next time I hug someone, I'll keep that in mind."

"Someone? What about me?"

"We've been over that," he practically growled. Why was it that he felt like he was on the wrong side of his courtroom?

"No, what you said is that you're not up for taking Ben's place. I've never once asked you to do that. You're making a huge deal out of nothing."

"Am I?"

The determined set of her jaw had issued a challenge. "You're the one freaking out over a simple—"

"I'm not freaking out. Here," he said, marching to the head of her bed, "is this what you want?" Before he'd gained enough sense to retreat to the kitchen, he'd perched beside her, wrapping his arms around her just like he'd been wanting to. The sensation was akin to easing into a sunlit pool. Easy, inviting and warm. Up close, she smelled so damned good. Like her flower-scented shampoo and lotions. After holding her a few agonizing seconds more, he tried releasing her, but she clung tight.

"Not yet," she said, her voice unwittingly hot and moist in his ear. "Please don't let go."

"Gabrielle…"

She'd shifted position, exhaling her every breath on his neck. What was she trying to do to him?

As she leaned closer, her soft curves met his solid frame, connecting them on a level that had him confused as to where he left off and she began. He didn't want to, but somehow all sanity escaped him, until he was leaning back, easing his fingers into her hair, pulling her in for a kiss.

Chapter Eight

"Whoa." Head spinning, lips tingling, entire body glowing, Gabby fought for air. Had Dane really just kissed her? Had she really enjoyed it more than any other kiss—ever? Had she secretly wondered if perhaps she'd hoped for something like that to happen when she'd demanded that damned hug? "Um… That wasn't in the hug description, but I like your technique."

"Sorry," he said, already away from her, safely in his favorite chair, gripping the arms tight enough to turn his knuckles white. "I never meant for that to happen." Leaning forward, elbows on his knees, he cradled his face with his hands. "It was a mistake. An accident. I—"

"Dane," she said softly, "it's all right."

"No, Gabrielle, it's not. You're my brother's girl, and—"

"I don't mean to interrupt," she snapped, "but do you see your brother anywhere in this house?"

"You know what I mean." As he lowered his hands, the look he cast her was heartbreaking. Tears shone in his eyes. As if he felt her stare, he looked away, and when their gazes next met the tears were gone. "My whole life has been based upon honor. Right and wrong. If you and I were to—"

He cleared his throat.

His vow to always be the responsible one weighed heavily on her. Only just now, in the unshed tears Dane hadn't wanted her to see, did she grasp the depth of his sincerity. He intended to do what was noble—whether it was what he wanted or not.

"I understand," she said, even though she didn't. She wanted to think herself capable of this level of self-denial, but doubted she was.

"Well, then…" He stood. "I'd better get back to supper."

"Right," she said, fumbling with her needlework tray. "I'd offer to help, but…"

Though he laughed at her feeble attempt to make light of the moment, she was no fool. It was written all over his face how badly he wanted to escape. Far be it from her to prevent him.

"HE KISSED YOU?" DURING THEIR Saturday afternoon gin rummy marathon, Olivia at least had the decency to look shocked by Gabby's confession. Dane was off playing football with friends.

From the foot of the bed, Stephanie clapped and giggled. "It's about time," she said. "What took him so long?"

Frowning, Gabby said, "Would you believe, honor?" After relaying the gist of Dane's speech, she added, "What are the odds that the only decent single man left on the planet has made a Boy Scout oath to never touch me?"

Nibbling a chunk of raw cabbage, Olivia asked, "How'd he kiss you if he's never going to touch you?"

"Good question," Stephanie said with another giggle.

"Oh, stop." Gabby threw her losing cards at them. "If you'd seen his face after the kiss—how disappointed he was in himself—you wouldn't be laughing."

"Aw, I'm sorry." Stephanie patted Gabby's feet. "I didn't realize you were serious."

"Of course I am," Gabby said, pushing herself up in the bed. "I wouldn't make up something like this."

Ever wise Olivia said, "The first night we met, I could tell he was trying not to be smitten with you."

"You could not," Gabby argued.

"Sorry," Stephanie interjected, "but I have to agree. You two seem made for each other. I can't imagine you with anyone other than Dane. He's the perfect grounding to your whimsy."

"My whimsy?" Gabby wrinkled her nose.

Olivia interpreted. "You drive a Jeep, he drives an Escalade. You're a massage therapist, and he's a judge. Your house is charming, and from what you've said, his home is intimidating."

"It's not all that bad," Gabby said. "Dane's house. I went to a holiday party there with Ben. In its present state it's a little austere and cold for my taste but it could be comfy. A little paint—warm hues—and some well-placed floral upholstered pieces, and—"

"Listen to you," Stephanie said, eyes wide with her hands curved over her bulging stomach. "One kiss, and you're moving in."

Olivia followed up with, "What shade have you selected for the new kitchen curtains?"

"Are you two here to visit or torment?"

"Visit," Olivia said, "but what's the harm in trying to knock some sense into you while we're here? Dane obviously adores you. Go for it."

"Go for it?" Now, Gabby was laughing, but not in a good way. "I've just told you that I already practically threw myself at him, as much as I could in this condition, anyway, and the man is too honorable to start anything with me. Yet your advice is to ignore his nobility in favor of what I want?"

"Then you admit to being attracted to him, too?" Olivia was further probing into what Gabby considered a private matter. She'd thought her friends would be mature about her confession. Instead, they'd just poked fun.

"It's not that simple," Gabby said. "Of course I have feelings for him, but they're complicated. You wouldn't understand. He's the brother of my baby's father. My even being attracted to him is wrong. Wrong, wrong, wrong."

Stephanie quietly asked, "Did it ever occur to you that you're the one who's mistaken?"

"What do you mean?" Gabby asked, notching her chin higher with self-righteousness on loan from her almost brother-in-law. "What could possibly be wrong about Dane and me having consciences?"

"Oh—I'll be happy to tackle that," Olivia said.

"No…." Swiping tears from her cheeks, Stephanie said, "I'll handle this one. You forget, I've loved a man and lost him. Michael is never coming back. He didn't just leave me, he's dead, Gabby. Dead. I'm not saying this to be cruel, but to remind you to live in the moment. I'd give anything to steal a few more days of happiness with Michael, and yet, here you are throwing away a chance at a brand-new life with a wonderful guy."

"But see?" Gabby asked, wiping a few of her own tears. "Even if I loved Dane—which I don't—how could I ask him to abandon his core beliefs…for me?"

"IT WAS JUST A KISS."

Dane glanced up from the brief he'd been struggling to read. "Excuse me?"

"Ever since we kissed, you've hardly spoken. You're here, but not really—if you know what I mean."

No, he didn't. Nor did he care to.

"It's Saturday night. Usually, we're having fun."

"Sorry," he grumbled. "I'm not in a fun mood."

"Because we kissed. And you feel guilty. But you shouldn't. We're both consenting adults and—"

Slapping his brief to his lap, Dane asked, "What in the hell has come over you? That kiss was a mistake. End of story. Why are you even bringing it up?"

"According to Stephanie, you—"

"You've talked to her about this?"

Nibbling her lower lip, she said, "Olivia, too."

"What's wrong with you?" he asked, teeth clenched. "This was a private matter."

Shaking her head, she said with a forced smile, "You afraid they're going to make a public announcement that might soil your flawless reputation?"

"Enough." He stood, uncaring that his brief fell onto the floor. Pacing the small strip of wood floor between the foot of Gabrielle's bed and the dresser, he said, "I don't give a damn what anyone outside my family thinks of me. If you knew me—really knew me—you'd get that fact."

"Dane, I—"

"Stop," he said, not wanting to hear what she had to say, because it wouldn't change a thing. "Did Ben ever mention a woman named Naomi?"

She shook her head.

"Not surprising." Pausing, he gripped the wrought-iron footboard, searching for what next to say. One part of him wanted to annihilate his brother. Show Gabrielle just what a snake Ben truly was. But another part of Dane wondered what purpose tattling on his brother would serve. Because Dane would never stoop to Ben's level in stealing an already-taken girl.

"What about her?"

"Nothing," Dane said. "Forget I ever mentioned it." Struggling to find peace within himself, he tried changing the subject. "Your nightgown is pretty. New?"

"Olivia and Stephanie brought it this afternoon." The ultrafeminine, filmy pink gown stayed within Gabrielle's princess theme, only this time she resembled a knocked-up royal who'd lost her crown. "Tell me about Naomi. Reading between the lines, I'm assuming you two were an item? Before she met your brother?"

"I don't want to get into this."

"Then why did you bring it up?"

"I don't know." Gripping the top of his head, he closed his eyes, wishing from the first moment his mom had broached the subject of him helping Gabrielle that he'd refused.

"Yes, you do. Because you wanted to tell me that what Ben did to you, you would never do to him. But what your Mr. Nobility brain left out of the equation is the fact that you didn't consciously *steal* me away from Ben like I suspect he did your Naomi. In watching over me, you've done everything right."

"Kissing you wasn't *right*. You don't belong to me."

"I don't *belong* to anyone, Dane! Believe it or not, I do have my own belief system and sense of right and wrong. What Ben did in leaving me—that was wrong." *Our kiss…was beautiful.*

Dane steeled himself against her words. What they'd shared for those few seconds had been amazing, but the sense of well-being had been an illusion. "Are you set for the night? Because if so, I need to get out of here."

"Dane, please don't go," she said, her voice raspy. "I'm sorry I said anything, okay? Let's just go back to the way things were between us. We were pals. We had fun. I promise I'll never bring up that kiss again."

From the room's threshold, he shook his head sadly. "Trouble is, whether or not you broach the topic, I'm not bloody likely to forget."

IT WAS FUNNY HOW EVEN THOUGH Gabby and Dane had only been living together a month, already they felt like a couple. At least she did—felt like *half* of a couple—despite his obvious wish for her to think otherwise.

Sunday, he hadn't been home all day, leaving her in the hands of his mother and grandmother. Monday, he'd practically thrown her breakfast at her in his rush to get out the door.

But today, lying in bed at five on a Tuesday morning, Gabby knew Dane's alarm was set for five-fifteen. Why on the quarter hour? Because he swore the extra fifteen minutes made all the difference on him getting enough sleep. She knew at 5:17 he'd shave, then grab a quick shower. On Monday, Wednesday and Friday, he went to his gym. But this morning, he'd linger, just a little bit. Just long enough to sit with her while she ate her blueberry bagel with cream cheese and drank a glass of OJ.

And then, once she'd finished and he'd taken her plate and glass to the kitchen, he'd return, asking her to check his tie—typically done in a flawless Windsor knot. She'd tell him it looked great. He'd thank her, fidget and make small talk for an awkward few minutes, and then he'd be off. His leaving had become her most despised part of the day, his homecoming the best.

"Would I be safe in assuming you want your usual?"

His question startled her.

"Um, sure," she said into the darkness. Most times, he would've at least turned on a lamp. "Thank you."

Her words had been wasted, as she already heard him banging around in the kitchen.

A few minutes later, he returned, flipping on the harsh overhead light.

In protest, her eyes refused to work.

"We're out of cream cheese, so I buttered your bagel."

"That's fine. Thanks." She swallowed the knot in her throat. Would things ever again be normal between them?

Wearing an imposing dark suit with a cobalt-blue

shirt and tie, he wasn't exactly looking his most welcoming best. Of course, he was incredibly handsome, but in an unapproachable way.

"You're welcome," he said, placing a serving tray on her lap. "I've gotta run, but Mom will be here around nine."

"It's only five-thirty. Why are you leaving so soon?"

"I've got a full schedule."

"Or you're avoiding me," she said around a bite of buttery bagel. Her frustration only made her that much more hungry.

"Don't be absurd." He crossed his arms.

"You made it a point to be gone all day Sunday, you left first thing yesterday morning and didn't come home till late last night. So late that you arranged for your mother to bring dinner."

"Your point being?"

"Duh. You're avoiding me."

"I don't have time for this." Turning to leave the room, he added, "Hurry up and eat. I'll take your tray."

"Please, Dane, talk to me. The doctor specifically told me to avoid stress, and your silent treatment is giving me indigestion."

Sighing, he said, "You're being melodramatic."

"From you, that's rich. I'm not the one pouting like a big baby."

"I don't pout." Nodding toward her tray, he commanded, "Hurry up and drink your juice."

"No. If you're going to act a quarter of your age in yelling at me, then I'll follow suit by going on a hunger strike."

Shaking his head, he snorted. "That's a laugh, seeing how Mom is bringing you baked ziti for lunch."

"Okay," she said, folding her arms, as well, "then maybe I just won't eat for you."

"Why are you doing this?" Sighing, he fell into his usual chair, resting his elbows on his knees. "At this point, you could go into labor at any time and your baby would be safe—just a little early. We're in the home stretch of our forced cohabitation. Can't you just allow it to end gracefully instead of on a sour note?"

"Love to," she said. "If you'd play nice, too."

"Okay…" He deeply inhaled. "I can't wait to hear what your expectations of 'nice' will be."

"For starters—" still starving, she bit into the second half of her bagel "—I could really go for another one of these. Who knew they were this good with butter?"

He laughed. Really, deeply laughed until he was wiping tears from his eyes.

"What's so *fwunny?*" she asked around her latest bite.

"If you had a mirror, you'd see."

Touching fingers to her chin, she asked, "Do I have butter all over my face?"

"Nothing so obvious. I just find it amusing how a few minutes ago, you were railing about how you never wanted to eat again, yet now you're demanding another bagel."

"I hardly demanded. I suggested."

"Uh-huh." Still grinning, he took her plate. "Be right back. Want more juice?"

"Yes, please," she said after finishing off her glass.

Upon his return, he sat again, only this time, he didn't seem under duress, but more like his usual self. Steepling his fingers, he said, "I owe you an apology. As much as I hate to admit it, you were right. I have been avoiding you."

Pausing midbite, in a quiet voice, she asked, "Why?"

With a sad chuckle, he said, "Damned if I know. I guess maybe because straight up, I am attracted to you. And I don't know what to do about it."

The honesty of his admission warmed her like a steaming cup of tea and honey.

"Do you have to analyze every little thing?"

After a moment's consideration, he said, "Yes."

Now she was the one laughing. "You're a mess."

"I agree." Rising, he grasped her free hand and said, "How are we going to fix me?"

"We?" She nearly choked on her bagel. "How am I supposed to know a magic cure?"

He brought her hand to his lips, kissing her whisper-soft. "It's your fault I have a problem."

"How?" she asked, pulse on a runaway course.

"Lying there, day after day, tormenting me with your cuteness. Pregnant, glowing you, wearing all of your cute, frilly, lacy, froufrou stuff. Disgustingly irresistible."

"Sorry?" She grinned. Never in her life had she felt more gigantic and unappealing, but far be it from her to disagree if that was the way Dane felt.

"You've turned my life upside down, and all you can say is sorry?" Stroking her palm with his thumb, he'd made all thoughts of anything but dizzying pleasure impossible. "I mean, seriously, Gabrielle, you're in my head. Even on the bench, I find myself wanting to call you—just to see if you're okay."

"And?" Was it wrong that learning of his so-called problem made her happier than she'd been in she couldn't remember when? "I see no problem with that."

"You wouldn't. But I never used to be this way." Releasing her, he paced. "I mean, my job was all I ever thought about. Well, and family, but they've never been all consuming. Nothing like you. And then there's that damned kiss…" He exhaled sharply.

"It was magical. Of course, that may just be my pregnancy hormones raging, but I'm pretty sure that even if I weren't pregnant, I would enjoy kissing you."

"But don't you see?" He stopped in front of the window. The sun was rising and dawn's glow slipped under wispy white curtains. "I shouldn't have kissed you. I broke my own honor code, and now I don't know how to live with myself."

Gabby wasn't sure what to say.

Dane's admission had thrilled her, but he was obviously upset. She thought he'd been on the verge of letting go of the ghosts Ben had woven through his life. She'd been wrong. He clearly wanted to let go, but refused. Which only made her situation all the more frustrating. "I am sorry."

He shook his head. "There's nothing to be sorry for. I made the mistake, and I'll deal with the repercussions."

What repercussions? Guilt? Regrets? She'd push the issue, but what was the point? He was hell-bent on taking the high road, and no matter how badly she craved his staying in her life even after her baby was born, she wasn't about to beg.

If he didn't want to be with her, then forget it. She didn't want to be with him.

Chapter Nine

"Thanks for taking me to the doctor," Gabrielle said Monday morning, squeezing herself into a waiting room chair at her obstetrician's office.

"No problem." It'd been a week since their morning talk, and on the surface, everything between Gabrielle and Dane seemed fine. But he knew the truth—he was torn up inside.

The office was packed with pregnant women. A TV in the corner had shown the same ten-minute prenatal care infomercial for nearly an hour. Dane could recite it.

The walls were green, the overstuffed sofas and chairs upholstered in dizzying stripes. As if the TV's drone wasn't annoying enough, sappy love songs played. Every side table was littered with pamphlets. *Your Baby and You. Baby's First Week. Breast-feeding Baby.* The air smelled like apples. The jury was still out on whether that was good or bad.

"I'm nervous," Gabrielle said.

Grasping her hand, Dane said, "Don't sweat it. You've been the perfect patient."

"Thanks to you." Eyes shining with emotion, she looked so pretty, Dane had to avert his gaze. That morning, he'd helped her with her hair. He'd fumbled through blow-drying and brushing. Burned himself twice with the straight iron. He'd helped her dress in black maternity slacks and a yellow, black and white smock-style blouse—looking away during the intimate parts.

He shrugged off her compliment. A few weeks, and all of this would be behind him. A good thing, right?

"What's got you so deep in thought?"

"A, um, case," he lied.

"Is it juicy, sad or infuriating?"

Laughing, he only just now realized he still held her hand. He tried releasing her, but she held on tight.

"I know it's juvenile, but please keep holding my hand. The comfort helps my nerves." She aimed a wobbly grin his way, and he was a goner. Of course he'd hold her hand. For however long she liked.

"What's this like for you? Being back out in the real world?"

"Overwhelming. I'd expected it to be exciting, but the traffic and noise and all of the people in here—it's a bit much." Leaning closer to him, she rested her head on his shoulder. Automatically, he raised his hand to comfort her, stroking her soft hair. "Being outside again was nice. In my yard. Feeling the sun on my face."

"You should've told me you were craving the Great Outdoors. I would've carried you to your front porch."

"You're sweet," she murmured, rubbing her hand absentmindedly along his chest.

"Gabrielle Craig," a nurse called.

"Guess that's me," she said, struggling to her feet. Dane stepped in to help, tugging her upright while she leaned forward.

He kissed her forehead. "Hope it goes well."

"You're not coming with me?"

"I suppose I can, but…" As he'd told himself all too many times, he wasn't the baby's father. He had no right to privileges like being with Gabrielle during private meetings with her doctor.

"Don't be a dork," she teased, taking him by his hand. "And besides, if you don't see the doctor, then you can't have a lollipop and sticker when it's time to leave."

"Why didn't you say so earlier?" Dane grinned. "I'd have already been back there."

After some small talk, the doctor bared Gabrielle's enormous belly, then waved a goop-slickened wand over the baby to listen for his heartbeat. Soon the room was filled with what sounded like a horse's gallop. Emotion knotting Dane's throat, he asked, "Is it normal for the little guy's pulse to be so fast?"

"Absolutely," the doctor assured. "Fetal heart rates are speedy. Anywhere between one-twenty to one-sixty beats per minute. Your little guy is clocking in at one-forty-four."

Dane started to correct the doctor's mistake in thinking the baby his, but didn't. Hearing that heartbeat had washed a proprietary wave through him. As much time as Dane had put into making sure Gabrielle's baby was healthy, he really did feel as if he was the infant's father.

"Isn't this exciting?" Gabrielle asked, reaching for his hand. When she laced her fingers between his, Dane's sense of well-being was electric. Being with

Gabrielle felt right. As if his life leading up to this point had been a dress rehearsal. This—now—was the real deal. But so was the fact that Ben was his brother. So were Dane's vows to never sink to Ben's level.

During the private portions of Gabrielle's exam, Dane ducked out into the hall, but a nurse soon called him back in. Though there were chairs in the cramped exam room, Dane preferred standing alongside the mom-to-be. Curving his hand over her shoulder, hoping she felt his support.

"I've got good news and bad," Dr. Yan said. Dane remembered the petite, kind woman from the hospital. A nurse dressed in Snow White–themed scrubs kept busy at the small counter, cleaning up the supplies the doctor had used. "Which would you like first?"

"Bad," Gabrielle said, a frown creasing her forehead.

"Relax." Dr. Yan gave her an easy grin and a pat to Gabrielle's feet. "Even the bad isn't all that traumatic. You're still two centimeters dilated, but in cases like yours, that's common. The good news is at thirty-three weeks, even if you went into labor today, your baby would most likely be fine—maybe a pound or two smaller than we'd optimally like."

"That's all good news," Gabrielle said with a relieved sigh. "The way this kid has been kicking, I thought you were about to tell me I'd be giving birth to a third-grade soccer star."

Laughing, making notes on Gabrielle's chart, the doctor said, "Not quite. Maybe just a second-grader." Finishing her notation, she added, "In all seriousness, you and your baby are doing great. Meaning the real bad news is that in a few short weeks, all of the pampering you've been getting is about to stop, and the work of caring for this little guy is about to begin."

"After lying in bed so much," Gabrielle said, "I'm actually looking forward to caring for someone else."

The doctor laughed. "All right, then. Unless there are problems, the next time I see you will be in another two weeks."

"Oh—" Struggling to sit up, Gabrielle said, "I forgot to ask, a good friend of mine's birthday is Friday. If I do nothing but sit, would it be all right if I attend her party?"

"You mean Mom's?" Dane asked.

"Duh," Gabrielle snipped. "It's not like I've seen anyone else who's having a party."

"Did I say you had?" Dane happened to glance at the doctor only to find her smiling. It irked him to see that she'd found their spat amusing.

Clearing her throat, the doctor said, "By all means, go. Just don't overdo it by dancing on any tables."

"Maybe just one," Gabrielle said with a wink.

"Seriously—the second you get into the home where the party is being held, I want you stretched out on the sofa."

Dane helped her scoot off the exam table, then ushered her to the office's checkout counter.

Outside, blue skies had turned gray. It was forecasted to rain that night. The temperature was in the muggy high eighties, with hardly a breath of wind stirring the newly built clinic's manicured grounds.

Helping Gabrielle into his car, Dane asked, "So Mom's having a big party, huh?"

"Just family. I think she mentioned your uncle Tommy and Aunt Frieda are coming."

"Swell." He fastened her seat belt. "The last time Uncle Tommy came, he brought enough homemade wine to leave Nana with a three-day hangover."

"He did not," Gabrielle said, giving him a playful swat.

"I didn't say he did, I said his wine did." He winked before shutting her door.

"Mmm," Gabby said, finally back in her pj's and climbing into bed. "Who'd have thought I'd actually miss lying down?"

"You've had a busy day. Getting dressed, walking fifty feet, taking a car ride…" Dane grinned.

"You're awful." She pulled up the sheets and quilt. Scowling, she asked, "Why are you being so mean?"

"Oh, I'm hardly being mean," he said, handing her a glass of cold milk. "Want cookies to go with that?"

"Yes, please."

While he was gone, Gabby fiddled with her pillows, trying to arrange them just right. Finally comfortable, she leaned back and closed her eyes. What a fun afternoon it had been. And how hard up was she for entertainment when a routine trip to the doctor was major entertainment? Dane had been the perfect companion. Funny and supportive and—

"Here you go, Your Highness." The saucer he handed her held three peanut-butter cookies. His mother had made them, bringing a dozen with yesterday's lunch.

"Thank you," she said with a sweet smile. "And from

now on when you address me, please use Queen Gabby. It's my preferred title."

Shaking his head, he asked, "Your Royal Pain in My Behind, what sounds good for dinner?"

"Since you asked, I've really been craving steak. Feel like firing up the grill?"

"For you—" he leaned over to kiss her forehead "—absolutely. Do you have a gas grill or charcoal?"

Drawing her lower lip into her mouth, she said, "I'm afraid of the former. Is that okay? Ben was always telling me to get a real grill."

"I prefer charcoal," he said. "I'll pick some up at the store. Need anything else besides steak and all of the trimmings?"

For you to kiss me again—only this time on the lips!

Fearing her face was as red as it was hot, she looked away. "That sounds great. Thank you so much."

"My pleasure." He looked at her for a long time, like he wanted to say or do something more, but wouldn't.

"Well…" Gesturing toward the door, he said, "Movie magazines? Candy? Anything?"

"What I'd really like is to go with you," she said wistfully. "You know, just be normal together."

"Hey," he said, instantly by her side. "What could be more normal than us?"

"Whoa—" She gripped her belly. "I was beginning to think I was dreaming this, but I swear the baby has started kicking more whenever you're beside me."

"No way," he said, cupping his hand over her belly's peak. Further proving her point, the baby kicked. Twice! "Holy crap. Make him do it again."

"Dane, I can't order him to kick for you."

"I know," he said, "but you said this has happened before, right?"

"Well, yes, but it's not on command."

"But you really think he knows me?" She'd never seen Dane so excited, which in turn made her feel the same. "So, like, after he's born, he'll recognize me?"

"According to the books, that's what happens," she said, putting her hand over his.

The baby kicked again. This time for both of them.

Their gazes locked, and if Gabby's heart hadn't been beating so fast, she'd have sworn it stopped. She felt disconnected from herself—as if she were conscious in a dream.

"I should get going," he said.

She nodded. *Please kiss me first.*

"So, I'm just going to go."

"Bye…"

He moved in closer and closer until his breath warmed her lips. "I'm leaving." Closer and closer. And then he stopped, lightly shook his head and slowly broke her heart by backing away. "Be right back, 'kay?"

Swallowing a knot of disappointment, she nodded.

"WAKE UP, PRINCESS GABBY."

When Gabrielle just murmured in her sleep and rolled over, Dane fought the urge to climb into bed beside her, hold her close and see if the baby would kick for him again.

Instead, he sat on the bed, just drinking in the sight of her. Four or five weeks, and then all of this would end.

She'd no longer have need of him. Oh sure, he'd help out with the baby every once in a while, but he wouldn't live here. Things wouldn't be like they were now. Like they were a couple.

She stirred. "Dane?"

"You were expecting someone else?"

Her voice all sleepy-sexy, she laughed. "Maybe. I never know when Brad Pitt might stop by."

"Mmm-hmm. He'd better not."

"Or what?" she teased. "You going to challenge him to a duel for my honor?"

"You never know," he said with a shrug. "What I do know is that I have two gorgeous T-bones ready to go on the grill. Hungry?"

"Starved." Holding out her arms, she said, "Carry me to the deck? I can recline on one of the lounge chairs."

"I would, but while I was heading home from the store, I heard thunder."

"I haven't. Please?" She wiggled her fingers. "I promise if it rains, you can haul me right back in."

"Gee, thanks," he said, already scooping her into his arms. "It'd be my pleasure."

Twenty minutes later, Dane had installed Gabrielle in a lounger and started the grill. The scent alone had his stomach growling. Far-off thunder rumbled and the sky looked grouchy but dry.

"It's nice out here," Gabrielle said.

"If you like muggy and buggy," he complained, swatting at a fly. Gabrielle's backyard was lush and overgrown; the oaks and maples had arched together, forming a canopy of green. "Your grass needs mowing. Your neighbor to the south has been doing the front."

"How sweet. I wish he'd come inside for a sec so I could thank him."

Shaking seasoned salt on the steaks, Dane said, "In a little over a month, you can thank him yourself."

"Oh, yeah," she said with a wide grin. "I forgot."

"You're a mess." Before putting the steaks on the grill, he swatted at another fly.

"And you're great for my ego." She stuck out her tongue.

"Sorry. I'm a judge—sworn to tell the truth."

She rolled her eyes.

They kept up their banter until the steaks were done. Dane put them on a clean plate, covered it with foil, then removed the foil from the pan of zucchini he'd already sliced lengthwise and soaked in olive oil and a few spices while Gabrielle had finished her nap.

"That's pretty fancy," Gabrielle said as Dane placed the thick slices on the grill. "Why haven't you shown off these skills before?"

"You've never asked. Prior to tonight, I thought mozzarella and butter were the only food groups you enjoy."

Feigning a growl, she said, "You'd better be glad I'm still stuck lying down or you'd get it, buster."

"*Oooooh,* I'm so scared." As if on cue thunder rolled. "Damn," he said, grinning toward the sky, "I couldn't have planned that better."

"You're the one who's a mess," she teased. "At least I'm not talking to the heavens."

The argument over who was the bigger mess continued until more ominous thunder forced him to hurry. "If it starts raining, want me to save you or dinner?"

"Dinner," she said without hesitation. "You can't towel-dry that delicious-smelling zucchini."

He nodded. "Duly noted."

Dane had just taken the last of the vegetables from the grill when the sky opened.

"Save the steak!" Gabrielle shrieked, holding the seat cushion from the chair beside her over her head. She was laughing and already soaked, as was he. Per her request, he ran dinner inside before returning for her, but just as he was opening the back door, she tottered her way inside.

"What are you doing up?" he scolded, holding the door open, urging her inside.

"It dawned on me that I am able to walk, I'm just not supposed to. But seeing how I have to use the bathroom anyway, I figured what would a few more steps hurt?" Dripping wet, her hair hanging in inky rivulets on her shoulders, she grinned up at him.

"You do know I'm going to have to yell at you, right?"

"Not necessarily," she said, already heading for the bathroom. "You could pretend you don't see me."

"Ah." He nodded. "The old invisible-pregnant-lady trick. Works every time."

"If I weren't so wet and miserable, I'd stop to let you have it." In the house's air-conditioned chill, her teeth chattered.

"Yeah, well, hold that thought while we get you into dry clothes."

Urging her to have a seat on the closed toilet lid, he

wrapped one towel around her head, and then handed her another. "Don't move. I'll be back."

"You're wet, too," she pointed out, teeth still chattering.

"You think?" After dragging off his wet T-shirt, he tossed it in the sink.

Gabrielle followed suit.

"What're you doing?" She sat there in her bra, towel-drying her hair. The sight of her full breasts and even fuller stomach left him speechless. She was beyond beautiful. With everything in him, he wanted to kneel in front of her, curving his hands around her belly. He wanted to kiss her. Not just on the lips, but all over. He wanted to taste every inch of her, feel every inch of her, know her body as well as he did his own.

"I'm changing." Her expression was matter-of-fact, making him feel like a gaping twelve-year-old for even caring. "After all the time you've put into keeping me healthy, do you really want to lose me from something as senseless as catching my death of cold?"

At least then they'd be even, seeing how he was currently on the verge of dying from need. He had never wanted a woman more. Never had he been more achingly aware of the fact that she wasn't his.

Chapter Ten

Only after Dane had left to get her fresh clothes did Gabby dare breathe. Good Lord, was his chest gorgeous. Well defined with just enough hair to make him manly without being a Sasquatch. The thought made her smile, as did the memory of his broad shoulders.

He returned wearing dry khaki cargo shorts and nothing else. With his dark hair all spiky and wet, a hint of stubble shadowing his squarish jaws, he was stunning. Gone was the formal judge. In his place was a rugged man whom she'd be all too happy to have jump her bones. But then, like he'd really want to. After all, with her being grossly pregnant, she wasn't exactly looking her best.

Presenting her with a pile of dry clothes, he said, "I wasn't sure if you were wet all the way through, or just on top."

Cheeks flaming, Gabby's already naughty mind didn't need much encouragement to take Dane's innocent question the entirely wrong way. "All the way through, thank you."

"Sure." Politely looking away, he asked, "Need help?"

"Probably, but I don't want to put you in an awkward spot."

"What do you need me to do?"

Again, Gabby found herself giggling. If she told uptight Dane what she really needed him to do, he'd pass out! "First, help me up from here."

He did, but instead of grasping her hands as she'd expected, he awkwardly took hold between her elbows and forearms, placing her face square in the center of that chest she'd admired earlier.

Once she was standing, Gabby wrapped her arms around Dane's waist for support. "I seem to have lost all sense of balance."

"Normal, I suppose, considering you have a watermelon where your waist used to be."

"You are so good for my ego," she said, shimmying free of her wet pj bottoms.

She was trying to be efficient. Clinical. She was trying not to notice the way her bare skin brushed his. And in the places where they touched there was fire. Her insides felt quivery and Baby Günter kicked as if he were in a championship soccer match.

All too soon, she had on her fresh yellow flannel pj's.

"There you go," Dane said, urging her toward her room. "Come on, let's get you back to bed and I'll fix you a plate."

"Thank you for your help." In the cramped, dark hall, she turned to him, flattening her hands against his chest. The wood floor chilled her bare feet. Dane's warmth counteracted all discomfort. On her tiptoes, she kissed his cheek. "You've been so kind—through everything."

She kissed his other cheek, and his chin.

Groaning, he warned, "Gabrielle…"

Turning her attention to his throat, and then lower, she said, "Please hold me. Please, don't make me beg."

"I can't—"

"It's just us, Dane." Skimming her fingertips along the dark curls on his chest, she said, "Ben's miles away. Don't let his ghost ruin what we share."

"What exactly is that?" he asked, resting his forehead against hers.

"I don't know," she said. "It's not anything I can define, but surely you feel it?"

"I'm not sure what I'm feeling anymore. Watching you started out to be the right thing to do, but now I don't just want to be with you, I *have* to be with you. And when the baby comes—"

"You'll still be here with me, right?"

He tried backing away from her, but she held on for dear life. "Let me go. You know it's for the best."

Arms around his waist, she said, "No, Dane, what I know is that I've never been happier than these past weeks with you. If it helps, you're hardly stealing me from Ben. I'm choosing you over him. Now I see he was a joke. You, Dane, are the real deal."

She kissed his chest. Over and over, pressing her lips to his skin, but then he braced his hands on each side of her face, forcing her gaze to lock with his. As if agonized over a war of will raging within him, he groaned again. But then he kissed her, and there was no hiding the depth of his emotions.

"What are we doing?" he eventually asked.

"Enjoying ourselves?"

Her matter-of-fact statement must have been just the right answer because he laughed before sweeping her off her feet and settling her back into bed.

"Comfortable?" Dane asked, pressing a soft kiss to her forehead.

She nodded.

"Need anything?" he asked in a throaty whisper. "Water... Extra pillow... A cookie?" Perched on the side of the bed, skimming her hair, he stared at her. Expectantly. Like maybe he needed something, but wasn't sure what. His warmth alongside her felt good on the chilly night.

Smiling, she shook her head.

He rose, taking his warmth with him. "All right, then. I, ah, guess I'll head to my room."

"O-okay." Something about him in the dreamy lamp-light made him almost unbearably handsome. His unread-able eyes, mussed hair and whisker-stubbled jawline. Was it wrong for her to want for nothing more than him to stay?

At the door, he said, "Remember, if you need any-thing—anything at all, I'm right down the hall." He hooked his thumb in that direction.

"That rhymed," she couldn't resist teasing with a giggle while trying to still her racing heart. "All—down the hall."

Curiously sober, he said, "You know what I mean."

Swallowing hard, she nodded. Boy, did she. Which was why she summoned her every ounce of courage to take him up on his offer. Shyly patting the empty side of her bed, she asked, "Stay? Please? I'll behave...." Flashing him a smile, she added, "I just don't want you to go."

Faintly smiling back, already headed her way, he said, "Me, neither."

"HAPPY BIRTHDAY!" GABBY SAID to Mama Bocelli Friday night, handing her a bouquet of two dozen hot-pink roses and a box of candy. The house smelled heavenly—rich with tomato sauce, Italian sausage and, of course, all sorts of cheeses. When Gabby's stomach rumbled in anticipation, the baby kicked.

Mama refused the gifts and shrieked, "What are you doing out of bed?"

"Relax," Dane said, taking the flowers and chocolates, then setting them on the hall table. "As long as she lies on the sofa ASAP, she has her doctor's permission. I heard it myself."

"That may well be," Mama said, "but you're under my care now, and I say you shouldn't be up."

"What're you doing out of bed?" Nana asked. She'd entered the room arm in arm with a well-dressed, silver-haired man. Nana was wearing her best red dress and must've just had her hair done as it was teased into a shellacked pile high on her head. "Go lie down."

Nana let go of the man Gabby presumed to be her Flavor of the Month and ushered Gabby into her purple recliner.

"Don't get up again," Mama said, pulling the lever that made the footrest pop out.

Sighing, Gabby looked to Dane for rescue, but he merely smiled and shrugged.

"Some help you are," she said to him under her breath while Nana and Mama fought over whether or not Gabby needed a blanket.

"They scare the hell out of me," he muttered. "I'm staying out of it."

"You're a wise man," Dane's father said, strolling up behind his son. "I avoid your mother as much as humanly possible."

"Me, too," Uncle Tommy said, a clear plastic tumbler filled with red wine in one hand and a thick wedge of garlic toast in the other.

Aunt Frieda had joined the great blanket debate.

An hour later, seeing how Mama still wouldn't allow Gabby to leave her recliner, the entire party had moved to the living room. From TV trays, they ate lasagna, spaghetti and meatballs, fettuccini alfredo and homemade creamy Italian-dressed salads. Dane's father had wanted to watch ESPN during dinner, but since it was Mama's birthday, her vote was the only one that mattered. *Breakfast at Tiffany's* was showing on TCM.

After the main course, there was tiramisu and singing before Mama blew out the candles on her birthday cake. She had four wrapped gifts. One was a new diamond watch from her husband.

Hands over her mouth, eyes shiny with tears, in a rare show of emotion, she kissed Pops full on his lips. "Thank you, Papa Bear."

"You're welcome," he said, patting her ample behind. *Papa Bear?* Gabby mouthed behind her hand to Dane.

He laughed.

Mama then opened a new Sunday hat from Uncle Tommy and Aunt Frieda. It was big and pink with plenty of netting, sequins and silk flowers. Following that was a red bathrobe and matching slippers from Nana. Her date's gift was a brass butterfly that was a little dusty and tarnished behind the wings.

Nana blurted, "Wasn't that the same gift you gave Helen for her last birthday?" Earlier in the night, they'd all learned Helen was Arthur's former wife. Oops.

Glaring at her mother, Mama put the butterfly back in its box, and then rose. "Since I'm the birthday girl, I think all of the boys should do the dishes."

"Here, here!" Aunt Frieda said.

"Yeah, and once Dane's out of the room," Nana said, "I want the inside scoop on what our little Gabrielle and him have been up to. Have you seen the way she glows?"

"That's my cue to get out of here," Dane said under his breath. "Good luck." He patted Gabby's right shoulder.

"Now that he's out of the way," Nana said, parking herself in the recliner next to Gabby's, "give us some dirt. What have you two been up to?"

The kitchen phone rang. Gabby took it as her out. "Shouldn't you get that?"

"Nah—" Nana waved in that general direction "—that's what the menfolk are for. Now, has Dane proposed?"

"Wh-what?" Gabby struggled not to choke on her spit. Her back had really been throbbing, and now she had to deal with this?

"You heard me. Is he going to make an honest woman of you?"

Aunt Frieda cleared her throat. "Nana, would you like me to help you get ready for bed?"

"Bed?" Nana snorted. "Do I look like a nine-year-old to you?"

"Mama," Dane said, cordless phone in hand. "It's for you."

"Who is it?" she asked. "Nancy from down the street? I was just thinking she hadn't wished me a happy day, when for her birthday, I—"

"Mama," Dane repeated, complexion ashen as he stared at Gabby, "it's Ben."

THE BIG ITALIAN DINNER IN Dane's stomach roiled. Just hearing his little brother's voice made him want to punch a wall. So cavalier. Just shooting the breeze. Acting as if this was any ordinary call on any ordinary day. Forget the fact that the woman he'd knocked up and then abandoned was in the same room. Forget that Ben had not only put Gabrielle through hell, but their parents, as well.

"Why, yes," Mama said into the phone, "she is here. Want to talk with her?"

Gabrielle wildly waved her arms in the universal symbol for *no!*

"Thank you, son. I'd like to see you, too.…"

Still waving, Gabrielle was now also shaking her head.

"Yes, well," Mama droned on, "here she is…" Covering the phone's mouthpiece, she whispered to Gabrielle, "He says he misses you, and hopes you'll give him a second chance. Talk to him, sweetheart. All he wants to do is talk."

Dane said, "Mama, can't you see she plainly doesn't want to speak to Ben? For God's sake, she's trembling." He sat on the armrest of Gabrielle's recliner, slipping his arm around her shoulders.

"With excitement," Mama said. "Go ahead, sweetie. Talk to him. I told you Ben would come around."

"Mom," Dane ground out, teeth clenched, "stay out of this."

Forcing a deep breath, Gabrielle reached for the phone. "Ben?"

Not wanting to hear Gabrielle talking to his brother, Dane stood and left not only the room, but the house, which all of a sudden seemed far too small.

Out on the front porch, he took a seat on the top step. The air was nippy. Monday's storm had brought much cooler temperatures. The kids playing night tag across the street were wearing sweatshirts and jeans instead of their usual shorts and T-shirts.

The week had been idyllic. He'd for once let down his guard and allowed himself to fantasize about a life with Gabrielle and her son.

"Don't tell me you're just giving up?"

Great. Nana had burst out the screen door. "I've seen the way she looks at you, Dane, and clearly you're the winner."

"I wasn't aware there was a contest," he said.

"Bull." She smacked the back of his head. "I thought you knew better than to lie to your elders."

"Who says I'm lying?"

Sitting beside him, she said, "You are the most competitive person I know. You got that from me." Winking, she patted his knee. "Which is why you're marching right back into that house to rip the phone out of her hand."

"Nana…" He sighed. "It's hardly that simple."

"Damn straight. So what are you still doing out here?"

Laughing, Dane said, "You are something else. I really need to ask you for advice more often."

"I know." She flashed him a big smile. "But if it got to be a habit, I'd have to charge you."

"WELL?" GABBY ASKED DANE. The trip home had already seemed long and they'd only been in the car for three minutes. The dark cocooned them, lending a cozy feel that was false considering the night's big event. "Aren't you going to ask what he said?"

"Didn't figure it was any of my business." Dane tightened his grip on the wheel.

"For the record," she said, adjusting the heat to blast on her frigid feet, "it's very much your business. We're a team, you and I, and the last thing I want you thinking is that I wanted to talk to him."

"If you didn't, why did you even take the phone? Why not tell my mother to shove it where—"

"Okay, whoa," she said, resting her hands on her stomach, "I would never dream of telling your mother any such thing. Especially on her birthday. It obviously meant a lot to her that I talk to Ben, so I did. End of story."

Pulling the car to a stop at a red light, Dane glanced over at her. "Just tell me already. Is he coming back? Did he pour out some mushy, gushy apology that made you instantly forgive him, and—"

Unfastening her seat belt, Gabby leaned across the center console to kiss the man quiet.

The driver of the car behind them honked.

"Fasten your seat belt," he grumbled.

"Yes, sir." After giving him a sharp salute, she turned the heater to a higher setting.

"Knock off the sarcasm. This is serious, Gabrielle."

"Okay, here's how it went down. Yes, he apologized. No, I didn't accept it. Yes, he poured out a ton of stereotypical Ben-isms, no doubt carefully planned to tug at my heartstrings. Only they didn't. Want to know why?"

He stayed silent.

"Dane?" she verbally nudged. "Don't you want to know?"

"Does it matter?" He steered the car onto the still-busy expressway.

"Heck, yeah, it matters because the whole time I was listening to him, I was thinking about you." She took a deep breath. "I think I may be falling for you, Dane."

"What?" Glaring at her, he swerved onto the shoulder but quickly corrected his mistake. "Do we have to discuss this now?"

"I guess not," she said, digging through her purse for gum. She hoped if she struck a cavalier attitude about having just dropped the emotional time bomb that'd been ticking inside her that Dane might think her speech a joke. "Actually, forget it. We never have to discuss it again."

"That's not what I meant," he said. "I want to be able to look at you, and in this traffic, I can't."

"Fine. We'll talk when we get home."

"Great."

Ten minutes later, Dane pulled his car into her drive. He helped her out of her seat, across the yard and up the front porch steps. He unlocked the door, ushered her inside. All without saying a word.

Which was just as well, considering that Gabby didn't even want to look at Dane, let alone launch a heavy talk. Her back hurt, and she longed to lie down.

After a quick stop in the bathroom, Gabby struggled with changing into pink-and-white polka-dot pj's and then waddled to her bed.

"Why didn't you wait for me to help?" Dane asked, standing at her open bedroom door.

"I managed just fine on my own."

Sighing, he said, "The last thing I want to do is fight."

"Then don't." Gesturing toward her bedside lamp, she asked, "Would you mind turning that off?"

"Yes, actually, I would mind." He made himself at home in his usual armchair. "Now, where were we?"

"I was about to go to sleep."

"Not just yet. Now, back to what you were saying in the car. Your admission that you might be falling for me? Is that really how you feel?"

"No." Folding her arms across her chest, she said, "I don't know what made me say that. I must have still been on a high from too much birthday-cake frosting."

"Don't do this," he asked, leaning forward to take her hand. "If that's the way you feel, I'm okay with it."

"You're *okay?*" she shrieked. "Get out!"

"Calm down," he said, squeezing her hand, which she promptly jerked free.

"I will not. I essentially told you you've become—I don't know—an integral part of my life. And you had no response other than to nearly run us off the road."

"I'm sorry." He took her hand back and, no matter how hard she tugged, refused to let go. "You surprised me. That was the last thing I expected you to say."

"You think I planned to say it?" Let alone feel it? With her free hand, she swiped away hot, messy tears.

"Then what do you want to do?" Stroking the top of her hand with the pad of his thumb, he said, "I'm in uncharted waters here. I've never been any good at this sort of thing, so you're going to have to show me the way."

"That's ridiculous," she said, refusing to even meet his gaze. "You're either attracted to me, or you're not. There's nothing mystical about it." Reaching for a tissue, she added, "Get it over with. Tell me you don't feel a thing for me other than pity."

Chapter Eleven

"Nothing could be further from the truth," Dane said, fury streaking through him. "How could I pity you when I admire the hell out of you? A lot of women faced with your situation would've crumbled, but here you are, still going strong."

Struggling to reach for the bedside lamp, she said, "Please just leave. My back really hurts, and—"

"Are you mental?" He thumped the heel of his hand to his forehead.

"Now you're calling me stupid?" She sat up, only to wince with pain that made her lie back down.

"Woman, can't you tell you're in labor?"

"No, I'm not. My back hurts. No doubt because of your mother and her stupid recline— *Ooooooh!*" Sweat beading her forehead, she rode out the pain before saying, "M-maybe you're right."

"Let's not panic," he said. "Let me grab my watch, a pen and some paper, and then I'll time you." In his room, he struggled to follow his own advice. Though her baby would most likely be all right if born this early, he didn't see the point in tempting fate. Armed with all of his contraction-timing supplies, he headed back to her room, mumbling, "I knew we shouldn't have gone to my mother's birthday."

"You think that's what started this?" she wailed. "I'll t-tell you why—ouch—I'm hurting, Dane. Because of you. You know I'm not supposed to have any stress, so you could've just told me you like me, too. But *nooo,* you had to be stubborn, even though I know you feel something more for me than nice, safe, platonic friendship."

"What if I do? It doesn't change anything," he argued right back, making note of her latest contraction. "Especially now that Ben's back in the picture."

"Back?" Laughing, she said, "I don't even know what state he's in. How is that the same as him being here, with me, taking care of me—like you?"

Sighing, he said, "This conversation is going in circles. Of course I have feelings for you. Affection. Something appropriate for a sister-in-law."

Looking away from him with an expression of disgust, she said, "Dane Bocelli, you're a lot of things, but I never took you for a liar."

"Whatever," he said, taking the remote from her nightstand and turning on CNN. "Believe what you want. I'm done with this argument. You know where I stand."

The question was, did he? Because the kisses they'd shared had felt anything but sisterly.

Gabrielle gave him the silent treatment until she fell asleep. Her contractions had no discernible pattern, making him think they'd been the harmless Braxton Hicks variety they'd learned about during Lamaze.

He turned off the lamp, trying to make himself comfortable in his chair. If this were his house, he'd buy himself a nice, roomy leather recliner. Redo this pink palace in a nice, manly navy and brown. Alas, it wasn't his house, and judging by Ben's call, it wouldn't be anytime soon.

SATURDAY MORNING, GABRIELLE woke to sun streaming through the openings in her filmy curtains. After wiping sleep from her eyes, she looked to her right to find Dane squashed into an uncomfortable position in his usual chair.

She needed a trip to the bathroom, so she tossed back her covers and went to him, giving him a gentle shake. "Wake up, or you'll need a chiropractor."

He was slow to open his eyes, and once he did and realized she was standing over him, he said in a groggy voice, "Why are you out of bed?"

"On my way to the ladies' room, warden."

He straightened, wincing while rubbing his neck. "Carry on, and then get back to your *cell*."

Once she'd returned, he was still in his chair, cradling his forehead in his hands.

"Thank you," she said, crawling into bed.

He looked up. "For what?"

"For keeping watch over me." Head bowed, she added, "I'm sorry. Our argument last night was silly. I know you care for me. Your actions tell me every day."

He replied with a shrug.

Eyes bloodshot with dark circles underneath, he looked exhausted, and she was the cause. If she were healthy, she'd urge him into her bed. Nap with him until he was well rested. She'd make him a breakfast. Waffles and bacon and fresh-squeezed juice.

"Can we please return to the way we used to be?"

With a sarcastic chuckle, he said, "Haven't you already asked me that once before?"

"Yes, but…" What could she say? That maybe this time would be different even though she knew it wouldn't? At the heart of their every argument was the fact that Dane would never betray his brother. It didn't matter that with each passing day she spent with Dane, Ben was driven further from her memory. Dane's pride would never allow him to give in to their mutual attraction. And no matter how vehemently he protested, judging by his kisses, it *was* mutual.

ANOTHER WEEK PASSED AND then another. Gabby wished for the same easy camaraderie she and Dane had once shared, but it truly seemed there was no going back. Oh, he was achingly polite, but distant. No more hugs or kisses. Precious few shared laughs.

When he came home Wednesday night of her thirty-fifth week of pregnancy, it destroyed her when he wouldn't even look at her while asking if she was all right.

"I'm fine," she said. "Bored. Sit with me?"

He tossed the mail onto her belly. "I would, but it looks like you have some reading to catch up on."

She picked up the first envelope in the stack. The return address simply read *Ben*. It had been postmarked in Los Angeles.

Dane's expression was thunderous. A muscle ticked in his jaw.

"You don't think I wanted this, do you?"

"It's none of my business," he said, leaving the room.

"Dane!" she hollered. "Please come back."

He didn't.

Hearing him rummaging in the kitchen, banging pots and pans and cabinets and the fridge door, she opened Ben's letter. Withdrawing a sheet of yellow, lined legal paper, her hands shook. Quickly skimming, finding herself not even caring what he'd written, she saw the usual apologies. He said he would try making it home for their child's delivery, but he couldn't make any promises. Wasn't that just like him? Sitting out in L.A., thinking she was back home wringing her hands while waiting for his return?

She called out again for Dane.

"What?" he asked from the threshold to her room.

"Remember how I used to talk about Ben in the present tense? As if any second he'd walk through the door?"

Arms folded, he gave her a barely perceptible nod.

"Well, after reading this, I'm angry enough to firmly put your little brother in my past." Holding out the letter to him, she said, "Take a look."

He took the letter, sitting in his armchair to read it. From time to time, he'd raise his eyebrows, as if surprised by his brother's words. Finished, he set the offensive piece of paper on her nightstand. "Classic. I especially enjoyed the part where he says he can't promise he'll make it back in time for his son's arrival into the world."

"Me, too," she said, liking the fact that for once they shared something in common. "What's for dinner?"

"Velveeta Shells & Cheese, a roasted chicken I

picked up at the deli and green beans. I wasn't feeling very inspired."

"It sounds delicious," she said, hating the exhaustion still marring his handsome features.

Shrugging, he said, "It is what it is."

"Dane?" she asked, voice soft. "Please tell me what's going through your head."

"Truth?" he said with a sad laugh. "I'm just wondering—if Ben does manage to make it back in time, who gets to be your coach? Him or me?"

"After all we've shared, how could you even ask such a thing?" Sitting up in the bed, she added, "Ben doesn't know the first thing about Lamaze. You're being ridiculous."

"Am I?" he asked. "You wanted to know what was on my mind, so I told you. It's a logical-enough question."

"Not for me." Swallowing the knot aching at the back of her throat, she said, "I choose you."

Out of his chair, he went to her, resting his head on her belly. The baby kicked, and he laughed through tears. "I'm sorry," he said, wiping his cheeks, looking away as if he was embarrassed. He had no need to be, his genuine show of emotion only endeared him to her all the more. "This is way more than I signed on for. I never expected to care—you know, like your baby was mine, too. I can't stop thinking about both of you."

"And this is a bad thing, why?" she asked with a wavering smile.

He laughed, only this time, fully and freely, tossing back his head. "You are something else."

"Thanks." She smiled. "I'll take that as a compliment."

ONE MORE WEEK PASSED, bringing Gabrielle's baby that much closer to safety. Dane had done his reading, and knew that every day Baby Günter stayed in the womb meant one less possible complication for him at birth.

On an ordinary Thursday night, having had no further communication from Ben, Dane found his mood better than it had been in a while. The closer he got to Gabrielle's house, the higher his spirits. He'd planned a special dinner for her. A meat loaf recipe given to him by his secretary. She'd promised it was impossible to mess up. A good thing, seeing how just the other morning, Gabrielle had shared one of her happiest childhood memories that'd involved sitting around her family dinner table eating meat loaf, sharing conversation and laughter with the parents she'd so loved.

During the meal's prep time, Dane had hefted Gabrielle into his arms, carrying her toward the living room so that they could talk while he cooked. His precious time with her was ticking away, and he didn't want to waste a minute.

Once he'd placed the meat in the oven and his lumpy mashed potatoes were done, Dane stuck a bowl of frozen peas in the microwave, and then had a seat on the sofa.

Lifting Gabrielle's sock-covered feet onto his lap for a massage, he said, "All jokes aside, what are you leaning toward naming your little guy?"

"I thought about Benjamin—you know, after his father, but…" The mischievous sparkle in her eyes told him she was joking. "Actually, no disrespect to my father, but since his name was Ralph, I kind of don't want to go there." Looking toward the ceiling, with a faint smile, she said, "Daddy, if you're listening, I hope you'll understand."

"I'm betting he does. And might I add, I applaud your decision. These days, someone will pick on kids for not wearing the priciest jeans or sneakers. Sadly, even though Ralph is a perfectly fine name, I can see where it'd be like painting a target on the boy's back."

"Exactly," she said, patting her belly, "which is why I'm leaning toward my Grandfather's name, which was Jackson. I'll call him Jack for short."

"I like it," he said, "although, I have been thinking that Dane Jr. has a nice ring." When he winked, she tossed a pillow at him.

"DO YOU REALLY NEED ALL of this stuff?"

Saturday afternoon, Gabrielle looked up from her cross-stitching to see Dane holding up her favorite *Sounds of the Tropics* relaxation CD. She was now in her thirty-eighth week of pregnancy, meaning her son's arrival would now be welcomed instead of feared. Dane had been amazing—except for now, when he was being a typical man in not wanting her to overpack for what would hopefully be a brief hospital stay. "Remember how our Lamaze coach talked about soothing music being a proved pain reliever? You don't want me to be in pain, do you?" She smiled sweetly.

He added the CD to her ever-growing pile.

"Thank you." She blew him a kiss.

He grunted. "What else?"

"Did you already grab my slippers?" She counted off a section of lemon bar cookie on her pattern.

"No. Won't you want to wear them around the house until it's time?"

"Good point," she said, starting on her next row. "Did you—"

The doorbell rang.

"Hold that thought," Dane said on his way to answer the door.

The commotion and loud conversation alerted Gabby to the fact that Mama and Nana had invaded. She loved them both dearly, but they had a way of taking over whenever they arrived.

Clomping on the hardwood floors announced the duo's pending appearance in Gabby's room.

"There's my girl," Mama crooned, leaning over Gabby's bed for a big hug and kiss. "I brought you cookies and amazing news."

"Oh?" Gabby said, most interested in cookies.

Nana took a shower cap off her head. "Can you believe it? Not three minutes after we left Thom's Cut & Curl, it started to drizzle."

"You still look gorgeous," Gabby said, eyeing Nana's pile of shellacked gray curls.

"Thank you," Nana said, patting the side of Thom's latest creation.

Mama huffed. "Would you please hush about your hair and let me get a word in edgewise?"

"I would," Nana said, "but I already told you, I don't think Gabby's going to like your news."

"Nonsense." Taking Ben's photo from Gabby's

nightstand, Mama said, "Why wouldn't she think Ben being on his way home is anything but wonderful? After all, he is her baby's father."

"Um…" Hating the way her pulse sped up, Gabby dared to ask, "How do you know? Did he call?"

"Yes, ma'am." Before Mama replaced the picture, she wiped the glass with her sweater's sleeve. "And right as we speak, he's in Little Rock, staying with an old friend. I got the number, so just as soon as you go into labor, he'll come home."

"Swell," Dane said, arms folded where he stood near the door.

"Watch your mouth," Mama snapped. "Ben is this baby's father, and he should be here for his son's birth."

"I never said he shouldn't," Dane noted. "My problem is that if he's a mere thirty minutes away, why isn't he here now? Why wait until you give him a call?"

Rolling her eyes, Mama said, "Just for once, could you please stop being a Negative Ned? Your brother is finally doing right by Gabrielle. I should think you'd be happy."

"I'd be happy wearing this." Nana stepped out of Gabby's closet with one of Gabby's sexiest red cocktail dresses slipped over her purple velour jogging suit. "Old Edgar's ticker wouldn't stand a chance."

"AT LEAST THEY BROUGHT FOOD," Dane said after his family had thankfully left. He and Gabrielle shared the bed while eating spaghetti and meatballs, garlic toast and Caesar salads.

"I'm impressed," she said with a grin. "Look at you, being all Positive Paul. I like this change."

Casting her a dirty look, he ignored her reference to his mother's belief that he was always negative. What he was, was realistic. What was the point in sugarcoating the truth?

"Hey." Nudging his shoulder, she said, "Lighten up. I'm just teasing. Actually, I didn't find your mom's news all that great, either. In fact, the more I think about Ben's deigning to pop into town just in time for our baby to pop out royally ticks me off."

"Ditto."

"So…" Setting her plate on the nightstand, she rolled toward him. "What I propose is that we not even think about your brother until I start having regular contractions. Deal?" She held out her hand for him to shake.

He nodded. "But I'm still not happy about him stepping back into your life—especially not just in time to snatch all the glory."

Cupping Dane's whisker-stubbled cheek, she softly said, "In my book, you're the hero. Ben had his chance and blew it."

Edging forward, Dane kissed the tip of her nose. "How is it you always know just what to say to make me feel better?"

By FRIDAY OF HER THIRTY-NINTH week of what was starting to feel like a never-ending marathon of heartburn, swollen feet and peeing every three minutes, Gabby was more than ready to say hello to her son. Her doctor had given her permission to move around the house, as long as she didn't do jumping jacks or cartwheels.

Funny, but now that she was actually allowed out of bed, Gabby was so exhausted that she didn't feel like budging.

By the time Dane got home around six, bearing a supreme pizza, her back and neck ached, and she'd have given her favorite diamond earrings for a nice, long soak in a hot tub.

"You look beat," he said, perched on the edge of her bed. "Everything okay?"

"Eh." She gave him the wavering hand signal universally known for someone being so-so. "I hurt in places I didn't even know I had. Olivia and Steph are coming over tomorrow for a canasta tourney, but I don't know if I'm up for it."

Feeling her forehead for fever, he said, "Your temp is okay. Mom said Nana has been sniffling. Hope you're not coming down with something."

She shook her head. "I don't think so. My guess is that weighing three tons is finally catching up with me. I did a load of laundry today and felt ready to drop."

"Then why didn't you leave it for me?" Smoothing flyaway hair from her forehead, he said, "Just because your doctor gave you permission to occasionally be out of bed, doesn't mean you should go nuts."

Frowning while stabbing a meatball, she said, "I'd hardly call a single load of laundry major spring cleaning."

"Woman, how would I deal with being stuck with you for my entire life?"

Was he joking, or had his question been an offhand proposal? Testing the waters for what she might say? Pulse racing at the mere possibility of him having been serious, she decided to play it cool. "Lucky for you, you won't ever have to find out."

Leaning closer, he planted a tender kiss to her lips. "Lord help me, but with each passing day, I find myself wanting to stay with you more."

"Why don't you?" Because her heart couldn't bear losing Ben, and then Dane, as well.

Touching his forehead to hers, he sighed. "You know the reason. But I've been thinking, maybe once Ben actually does show, the two of us could have a man-to-man. I'd find out what his intentions are toward you."

Wrinkling her nose, she said, "You make me sound like medieval chattel."

"Sorry." He didn't look the least bit apologetic but determined to find a solution to his guilty conscience. "You know how I feel about stepping into Ben's territory. If we are given the opportunity to be together, I want it to be right."

"If talking with Ben would make you— Arrrrgh." She clutched her stomach.

"What's the matter?" he asked, voice rich with concern. "Mom's meatballs not settling well?"

"I know this will sound stupid, but I've been achy and crampy all afternoon, and what I just felt was more than that. You know, like a contraction. Do you think I might be going into labor?"

"It's possible," he said. "Your doctor said it could be any time now. Want me to make note of when you have a contraction?"

Nodding, she said, "Yes, please."

He took her half-eaten plate of food and set it on the

kitchen counter before gathering his official contraction-timing gear.

Back in his usual spot in her bedroom, he asked, "Did you have any while I was gone?"

"Uh-huh."

He wrote that down.

"Dane?"

"Yes?" He looked up from the notebook he'd purchased for just this purpose.

"What if we did something crazy like elope?" Because Gabby was afraid that if Ben did show up, Dane's sense of nobility would supersede whatever else he might feel.

"You mean now?"

"Sure." Wincing through another contraction, she said, "It'll be fun."

"No, it won't, because if your contractions keep up, we're not taking you anywhere but the hospital."

"Please," she begged. "I don't want to lose you."

"Honey, I'm not going anywhere." Rising, he curved his hands over her stomach, grinning when he felt a kick. "That is, unless you want me to."

"Then why won't you marry me?"

"Because you deserve a proper wedding with all of the trimmings."

Pouting and hurting, she said, "Sounds to me like the typical Dane put-off."

"You're being ridiculous, in fact—"

Ooooooh. "That one especially hurt." But not nearly as much as his rejection.

Chapter Twelve

Sure enough, Gabrielle was in labor. Dane had bundled her up for a trip to the hospital, and the nurse on duty had called Dr. Yan. Then she hooked Gabrielle to a fetal monitor and IV, took vital signs and brought around paperwork to sign.

"Okay," the nurse said while covering Gabrielle with an extra blanket, "now all you do is wait. Once you've gone into active labor, the real fun begins."

"How do I kn-know when I'm in active labor?"

"Oh, honey," the nurse said with a laugh. "Trust me. You'll know."

Once they were on their own, Dane pulled over a chair so that he could be by Gabrielle's side. There was so much he wanted to say. He hated that a special moment like this had been prefaced with an argument. Of course he wanted to marry her. But he couldn't. Not yet. "Need anything?"

"*Nooo…*" She grasped his hand, squeezing for all she was worth during her latest contraction.

When her pain had lessened, he went to the sink for

a washcloth. Running it under cold water, he placed it on Gabrielle's forehead, smoothing back her hair.

"I—I have something to tell you."

"Me, first," he said, easing alongside her in the bed. "I do want to be together forever. I'm sorry I wigged out on you."

A half smile lighting her eyes, she said, "It's okay. You're about to— *Rrrrrr…*" Her furrowed forehead served as a visual barometer of her pain.

"Whatever you have to say can wait. Let's just ride this out together."

Shaking her head, she managed to say, "It's about Ben. I didn't tell you everything he said on the phone when he called for your mom's birthday."

Stomach clenching, Dane said, "It doesn't matter. Nothing he said could change how I feel about you. I'm here for the duration."

"Th-that's just it…." Through gritted teeth, she continued, "H-he said that not only does he want to be here for our baby's birth, but he wants us to try being a family—you know, with the baby, and that—"

"Stop." Dane wanted to punch something. Instead, he dragged in a few slow, deep breaths. Odds were Ben had been making empty promises. It would be typical of him to tell Gabrielle he'd be here for her, and then fail to show. "Your worrying is wasting energy," he said, taking both of her hands into his. "The odds of Ben actually appearing for his own son's birth are, at best, remote."

"ARE YOU EXCITED?" STEPHANIE set the teddy bear and balloons she'd brought on the hospital room's wide windowsill. It was eight in the morning, and after a long night of ever-increasing pain, Gabby wasn't sure how much more she could take. Dane had been wonderful, but seemed nervous. Every time the door to her room opened, he jumped. When whoever was at the door wasn't his brother, he relaxed. Gabby had sent him out to eat breakfast when Steph had gotten there.

"I'm mostly scared," Gabby admitted, bracing for the next contraction. "E-everyone keeps telling me first-time deliveries are notoriously long."

"Swell." Stephanie sat hard in the room's only guest chair. "That'll be something for me to look forward to."

"I thought your sister had her first baby on the way to the hospital?"

"She did." Taking a bag of peanut M&M's from her purse, Steph ripped it open and held it out to Gabby. "Want one?"

"N-no, thanks." Usually chocolate was her friend, but today, just thinking about it made her want to puke.

"Anyway," her friend rattled on, "just because Lisa had her baby fast is no certainty for me—especially not with twins. So?" she asked through a fresh handful of candy. "What's got Dane looking so glum?"

Even the condensed version took three contractions to get through.

"Whoa." Stephanie stopped chewing long enough to take it all in. "So Ben could just show up at any minute?"

"Pretty m-much."

The door creaked opened, and both women looked to see who it was.

"Oh, hi, Dane," Gabby said. Months ago, she probably would've been thrilled at the prospect of Ben's return, but now, since getting to know Dane, she didn't care if she never saw him again.

Are you sure about that? her conscience inquired. *He is Baby Günter's father.*

"Don't sound so ecstatic." Dane closed the door behind him.

"I'm s-sorry." Holding out her hand, she said, "Please come here. I missed you. Stephanie's a bad substitute *c-cooooooach*."

With Dane again beside her, all of Gabby's worries faded, leaving her free to focus on breathing through her pain.

"Hey, I was an amazing coach," her friend protested before popping a few more M&M's.

A knock sounded on the door.

"Anyone home?" Olivia poked her head through.

"H-hi," Gabby said. "Th-thank you for coming."

"I wouldn't have missed it," she said, "although looking at you, you're not exactly a poster child for *Glamorous Birth* magazine." Snatching Steph's candy bag, she shook out a handful of M&M's.

"Y-you're lucky that's not a real p-publication, or I'd hit you over the h-head with it."

"No hitting," Dane ordered. "Remember what the doc said about watching your blood pressure."

"Has it been high?" Olivia asked.

Grim-faced, Dane nodded.

The room door opened again, only this time it was Mama Bocelli and Nana and her boyfriend, who carried

a portable folding chair, and Pops Bocelli and—
Gabby's heart caught in her throat.

"Look who I brought to visit!" Mama said, giving her
younger son a shove. "Aren't you excited to see Benny,
Gabrielle?"

"Whoo, hoo, hee, hee." Excited hadn't exactly been
the first word springing to Gabby's mind.

"Oh, baby," Ben said, instantly by her side, nudging
Dane out of the way. "Look at you. You look so sad." Ben,
on the other hand, looked as handsome as ever. Skin sun-
kissed, dark hair mussed, eyes as blue as the sky. He wore
jeans and a mossy green Abercrombie & Fitch T-shirt.
"Tell me what I can do to make you feel better."

Leave.

"N-nothing," she said.

"We need to talk." Dane grabbed Ben none-too-gently
around his upper arm and shoved him out of the room.

"Oh, dear," Mama said.

"Save my spot," Nana said, getting up from the seat
her boyfriend had lugged in.

"Where do you think you're going?" Mama asked,
catching her by the sleeve of her purple dress.

"To watch!" Nana jerked free, darting out the door
faster than Mama and her considerable girth could move.

Gabby winced in silent, screaming pain.

Olivia cleared her throat. "How about we all give
Gabby her privacy?"

"But we're family," Mama protested. "She wants us
here, don't you, darling?"

The pain was too intense for Gabby to talk. She was

hoping her agonized expression said it all. Plus, her bed was wet. Had her water broken?

"Of course she wants you here," Olivia soothed, nodding to Steph for help. "But I'm pretty sure she's ready for a rest."

"She can't rest in the middle of giving birth," Mama reasoned on her way out the door.

Pops and Nana's boyfriend trailed after her.

"Don't worry," Stephanie said to Gabby in a stage whisper, "we'll keep the whole Bocelli crew occupied."

"Th-thanks."

On her own, Gabby rummaged for the nurse's call button. She closed her eyes, wishing for a moment's relief from the pain. Then she might have a shot at clearing her head. Ben was home. He'd returned to care for her and the baby. She'd once wanted nothing more. Now she didn't know what she wanted other than for their baby to be born.

"Hey, hon, what do you need?" The nurse bustled in.

"I–I think my w-water broke."

Lifting the blankets, the nurse whistled. "You weren't kidding. Let me grab some fresh linens and I'll get you nice and dry, okay?"

Gabby nodded.

"Your doctor is on the floor. She'll be right in to check your progress."

Gabby nodded.

The nurse brought a colleague, and in no time, Gabby was cleaned up and dry.

Just as they'd finished, the doctor came in.

"Ouch," Dr. Yan said while consulting Gabby's

chart, "bet you're wishing you were back home loung-ing, huh?"

"Y-yeah."

"All right, well, let me take a look at what's going on with this kid of yours, and with any luck, you'll be resting comfortably with him real soon." Tossing the blankets back, she asked one of the nurses, "Becca, how about grabbing Gabrielle's Lamaze coach. He's right outside the door with another gentleman."

The nurse left.

Gabby's apprehension rose along with a fresh wave of pain.

"Ride it through." The doctor rubbed Gabby's knees. "There you go…. It'll pass."

Nodding, Gabby forced a deep breath.

The doctor took rubber gloves from a wall dispenser, and then, with the nurse by her side, performed her exam. Once finished, the doctor removed her gloves, made notes in Gabby's chart and then graced Gabby with a reassuring smile. "Well, we've got another good news, bad news situation on our hands."

Gabby groaned.

"Don't worry," the doctor said, "the good is that you're fully dilated. The bad is that you've got to get through one more rough patch before you're holding your son in your arms. You ready?"

"Do I have a—*chooooice?*" If Gabby had known having a baby hurt this bad, she would've told Ben to take a hike before their first kiss!

"Sorry, sweetie," her doctor said with another affec-tionate pat.

From out in the hall came the sound of raised male voices.

The doctor looked that way. "Last time there was that much commotion up here was during a heartbreaking adoption case when the birth mother changed her mind about giving her baby away."

Gabby wished the latest scuffle was so cut-and-dried. Not that she didn't feel for the adoptive parents' heartbreak, but at least their issue had an ending. She suspected her troubles with Dane and Ben were only just beginning.

Though his voice was muffled, she plainly heard Ben say, "Screw you, Dane. I'm the baby's father. You're nothing more than a freakin' Lamaze coach."

"Yeah, I'm also the one who picked up the pieces of the mess you made of Gabrielle's life."

"Gentlemen," Dr. Yan said, opening the room door, "this is neither the time nor place."

"Damn straight," Ben said. "I came a long way to be here, and I'm not missing my son's birth."

"But you had no problem missing the last nine months?" Dane pushed open the door with enough force to slam it into the wall. "Gabrielle, would you please tell my little brother that he's no longer needed?"

She wanted to, but how could she when Ben *was* her baby's father? Did she even have the legal right to ask him to leave? The pain was so great her mind was muddied. She could hardly catch her breath, let alone think. Why was this happening? Why couldn't Ben have come later? Better yet, not at all?

The doctor said, "While I change into scrubs, I'll let you sort this out."

Ben was at her side. "Tell Dane you don't need him anymore. I'm back, and I'm here to stay."

Dane stood at the foot of her bed, staring, staring until she felt his disappointment in her as certainly as a slap. The fact that Dane was the consummate gentleman and would never speak his displeasure only made his anger hurt that much more.

"*Daaaaane...*" She held out her hand to him. Her contractions were agonizing. All she wanted was for him to hold her, love her and tell her everything would be all right.

Still staring, only this time at Ben, Dane rounded the bed to stand next to her. "I'll be with you in spirit, but it's Ben who should be here."

Nooo, she wanted to scream, but she lacked the energy to fight. Besides which, the fact that Dane would willingly leave her after all they'd shared...

The pain was too much to bear.

Time ceased to exist. There were only more never-ending contractions. Pushing and gritting her teeth.

"Come on, babe, you can do it," Ben coached, acting as if he'd never been gone. Part of Gabby hated him for it. Another part, desperate for comfort, slipped back into her old routine of leaning on him. As the hours passed, so did the months Ben had been gone. She was half out of her mind with exhaustion. Maybe he'd never even left her? Maybe her time with his big brother had been but a wonderful dream?

Dr. Yan hurried into the room and took her place at the foot of the bed. "Push," she urged. "Come on, honey, I see your baby boy's head! *Push!*"

Two nurses were also there, coaching her on.

Ben never complained no matter how hard she squeezed his hand.

"There you go," the doctor said, "just a little more... You can do it. Push, Gabrielle, push!"

"Arrrrgh!" With all of her might Gabby gritted her teeth and pushed. And when her baby's head popped out, the relief was intoxicating. Like seeing the sun after days and days of gray.

The sound of her baby crying was music to Gabby's ears.

"Congratulations," Dr. Yan said, "she's a girl!"

"What?" Gabby bolted upright. "But I thought—"

"Relax," the doctor said in a laughing tone. "I was teasing. You have a perfect, healthy baby boy." And to prove it, suddenly her son's heart beat against hers. Tears sprang to her eyes, emotion bubbling inside her. Dane? Where was Dane?

"He's cool," Ben said, using just his index finger to stroke the infant's brow. "We made a good-looking son."

Her baby was everything Gabby had dreamed he would be. Ten tiny fingers and toes. A shock of black hair and his daddy's piercing blue eyes.

"He's got your nose," Ben said.

"Thank goodness," Gabby teased.

"If you don't mind," Dr. Yan said, "we need to cut the umbilical cord and then take him for some routine tests."

The doctor and nurses shot into action, cleaning not only the baby, but Gabby.

"Sir? Would you mind stepping out while we make your wife more comfortable?"

"Um, sure," Ben said, not correcting the nurse's mistake. He kissed Gabby full on her lips, and then asked, "You going to be all right?"

What a loaded question.

Fingers to her mouth, she couldn't ever remember being more confused. Couldn't he have allowed her a few moments' peace before messing with her already swimming mind?

"I—I'm fine," she managed to say.

"And I remember all too well that pouty look." Kissing her again, he said, "I'm going to leave you in the nurses' expert care, but when I get back, you're going to tell me what's going through your gorgeous head."

Chapter Thirteen

"Look what I've got," Ben said late that afternoon, carrying his blanket-swaddled son into Labor and Delivery's waiting area. He beamed with pride—as if he'd done so much to help bring the baby into the world.

As badly as Dane wanted to hold the infant who'd grown excited at the sound of his voice, he remained on the fringe of onlookers. His mother and Nana were oohing and cooing. Olivia and Stephanie each took a turn holding the newborn. Everyone was so concerned about the baby's well-being, but no one had asked about Gabrielle. How badly had her long labor hurt? Had she thought about him? Missed him?

He needed to see her. Even if she was sleeping, he needed to know she was all right.

Slipping away from the waiting-room crowd, he quietly entered her room. Wearing the pale pink pj's he'd packed for her, she looked finally at peace after the delivery that'd ravaged her body. He'd ached for her, wishing there was something he could do. Had his little brother even cared that she'd been in pain?

Consumed with regrets and resentment for Ben's arrival, Dane turned to leave. But then there was a small groan from the bed.

"Dane?"

Fighting the sting in his eyes, he turned to her, forcing a smile. "Hey. I saw your son. He's already quite the ladies' man."

She graced him with a drowsy grin.

"Are you all right?" he asked, stepping forward to take her left hand. "Was it rough?"

"As sandpaper," she quipped. "A-are y-you angry with me? About Ben being there instead of you?"

Yes. But now wasn't the time or place to show it. "It all happened the way it was supposed to. Leave it be."

"I—I wanted to fight for you to be the one sharing the birth with me. You deserved to be there. But the pain took over and I couldn't think. My body was on autopilot and I was just along for the ride."

"I understand," he said, even though he didn't. The rational side of him fully got the fact that Ben was her child's biological father. But there was so much more to being a great dad than just showing up in the delivery room.

"He is beautiful, isn't he." Her eyes radiated her contentment. Her complexion glowed. Her long hair tumbled around her shoulders in perfect disarray. She'd made a lovely pregnant woman, but was a full-on gorgeous mom.

"Yes, he is." Dane cupped her cheek, brushing silent tears with his thumb. "What's wrong?"

Shaking her head, she laughed through a teary

sniffle. "There shouldn't be anything wrong, but I can't stop thinking about how nothing went like we'd planned. All of those hours we spent in class, making sure my baby's delivery would be a calm, orderly process just sort of flew out the window."

"It's okay," he said. "The end result of holding a healthy child in your arms turned out the way we wanted. That's what's important."

"You always know the right thing to say. How can I ever repay you for all that you've done?"

"Bake me a few dozen cookies every now and then and we'll call it even." *And every day for the rest of my life, I'll wonder what I could've done to make this turn out differently.* To ensure that Ben never rode in to take the woman and baby that were rightfully his.

"Ben asked me to marry him."

The shock of her matter-of-fact confession took him a minute from which to recover. "Oh?"

"I told him I'd think about it. He hurt me. He wants to just sweep all of our troubles under the proverbial rug, but it's not that easy."

"No, I imagine not." Dane was not only proud of her for turning down his little brother, but filled with secret hope that maybe Gabrielle finally realized which of the Bocelli brothers was better husband material. How could she have forgotten that she'd first proposed to *him?* Why, why hadn't he just said yes? Because now, in the face of losing her, all of Dane's so-called noble concerns about not stealing his brother's girl seemed ridiculous.

Was he only imagining it, or had her contented

expression turned wistful? As if her fairy tale weren't quite coming true.

"Could you do me a favor?" she asked.

"Anything." Most especially if it had to do with telling Ben to take a hike.

"Could you please find your brother, and tell him I'd like to see my baby."

"IT SEEMS SURREAL," GABBY said, gazing upon the face of her son. Hours had passed, yet with a never-ending stream of well-wishing Bocelli aunts and uncles and distant cousins stopping by, this was the first time she'd managed to privately drink him in. Tracing his tiny nose and eyebrows and lips.

"What?" Olivia asked. She was Gabby's sole guest, and had sat quietly while working a crossword puzzle.

"Finally seeing him. He truly is a miracle. How this gorgeous little guy has been inside me all this time."

Olivia patted her still-bulging belly. "Hear that? Our friend Gabby says that pretty soon, I'm going to be as happy as she is instead of peeing every five minutes and suffering mind-numbing indigestion."

"It's worth it," Gabby assured.

"If you say so." Olivia's grin softened her sarcastic tone. "So, now that the whole Bocelli clan is out of our hair, what are you planning to do about Baby's daddy?"

"You mean Ben?"

"I'm not talking about the abominable snowman."

"Ha, ha," Gabby said, even though her friend's question wasn't the least bit funny. "I'm not sure what I'm supposed to do about him. I mean, he acts as if we're still a couple. During my labor, I didn't have the where-withal to tell him to leave, but now I'm regretting the fact that he was there...."

"Instead of Dane?"

Gabby sighed. "He's hurt. He's trying not to show it, but I can tell."

Toying with the ear of a baby-blue elephant one of the Bocellis had brought, Olivia said, "I don't blame him for being upset, but his brother had every right to be in the room."

"Every legal right," Gabby argued, "but what about morally? He abandoned me—and his son. If having babies were a sport, this would be like the quarterback showing up in the last thirty seconds of the game."

Olivia laughed so hard she snorted. "Oh, Gabby, you do have a way with words."

"YOU'VE THOUGHT OF EVERYTHING," Ben said upon walking into the nursery. He'd picked her and Jackson up from the hospital late that afternoon. After two nights in the hospital, Gabby couldn't wait to get home. On the other hand, would it even feel like home with Dane not being there?

"I tried," Gabby said, rocking Jack, who was cradled against her chest. He weighed only six pounds, ten ounces, but what he lacked in size, he more than made up for in spunk. Even at two days old, he seemed curious about everything and everyone he saw. Gabby was breast-feeding, and already the bond she felt for him was beyond any attachment she'd ever felt before. "But it was tough with me being stuck in bed for all those weeks. Dane picked up a lot of things I'd forgotten. He's really been great."

Scratching his head, Ben leaned against the changing table. "I know Mom roped him into being your Lamaze coach, but what's up with him camping here?"

Gabby had to count to ten in her head not to lash into him. "Your brother has been a godsend. I don't know how I would've managed without him."

"I'm sorry," Ben said. He grabbed the baby powder dispenser, twisting the lid open and closed. "Really. I had a lot of time to think in L.A., and the best I can come up with is that I left because I was scared."

"Of what?" Nuzzling Jack's downy-soft hair, she fought the knot in her throat. She wouldn't let him see her cry. "We were good together, Ben. Our love created this child. You ruined that. Just threw it away."

"You think I don't know that?" He slammed the powder bottle to the table. "Why do you think I left? It was too good. Something was bound to go wrong. I wanted to get out before it all went bad."

"How do you know it would've?" she asked, no longer caring that tears streamed down her cheeks. "How could you be so cruel as to not even have the decency to tell me your fears? I was carrying your baby. We could've talked it out. Gone to a counselor or something. You didn't even give us a chance."

He covered his face with his hands.

"Say something."

"Like what?" he asked. "I can't turn back time."

No. And truthfully, knowing what she did now, would she even want him to?

In front of her, he knelt, resting his hands on her knees. When they'd first met, his every touch was electric. She'd lived for his kisses. Now it wasn't Ben she craved, but his older brother.

"Please, Gabby," he said, "give me a second chance. I promise this time will be different."

"How can you make that kind of promise? You can't."

"All right," he admitted, "so I might fail again, but for the sake of our son, shouldn't we at least give us a try?"

ON A SUNDAY AFTERNOON, a week after Jack's birth, three days before an early Thanksgiving, Gabby stood in the Bocelli family dining room, staring out at the gloomy sky. A drizzle had set in, making the already turning leaves look dreary—especially the ones already on the ground. The temperature hovered in the teens. Cold for this time of year.

After having been passed around to the whole Bocelli clan both before the meal and after, Jack was out. He slept soundly in his portable playpen.

"Five bucks for your thoughts." Dane stepped up behind her, startling her from her introspection.

"That's a lot of money," she teased. "Deal." It was so strange being around him. Familiar, yet not.

He chuckled. "Guess I'd better check my wallet before making such a grand offer, huh?"

"Yep." A yearning crept through her. She missed talking with him and sharing meals and laughter and arguments and—

"You look pretty. New dress?"

"Yes, sir." He'd noticed. As she'd slipped into the ruby-colored suede dress, she'd wondered if he would.

"New hair, too. Looks like someone was ready to get out of the house." When he smiled, the familiar crinkles around his eyes made her ache with loneliness.

"I was," she said, "but it's different going out with a baby in tow."

"Better, I should think. Considering how handsome Jack is." He looked to his feet, then back to her. "I like the name, by the way. After your maternal grandfather, right?"

He remembered. "Yes. I never met him, but from the stories my mom told me, he was an amazing man." *Just like you.*

An awkward silence fell between them.

Dane broke it with a pointed question. "You and Ben together?"

"No," she said. "He's living in your old room, but that's the extent of it. He hurt me. I'm not yet ready to forget or forgive."

He nodded. Had there also been a faint sigh of relief? "For the baby's sake, you should. You know, give Ben a chance."

Just like that, you're giving up on us? On Jack? Had he already forgotten the nights they'd lain together, feeling the baby kick?

For the longest time, she stared at him, wishing she could see into his head.

"There you are." Ben sauntered up next to her, wrapping his arm around her shoulders as if he were staking his claim. "I wondered where you'd run off to. You're missing the game. Hogs are up by ten over Alabama."

"*Wooo* pig," she said. Whether you'd attended the

University of Arkansas or not, if you lived in Arkansas, you cheered for the Razorbacks.

"Baby—" Ben addressed her as if Dane weren't even in the room "—Mama wants to know if we're free Wednesday night. She wants us to bring Jack by her choir practice."

"Um, I guess that would be all right." Dane caught her gaze. With his deep brown eyes, she imagined him telling her he missed her. Too bad that in actuality, he'd already looked away.

"AS MUCH AS I LOVE BENNY," Nana said to Dane where he sat on the covered back porch steps, "he has no business being a dad. Did you see him fumbling to change Jack's diaper? He nearly dropped him on his head." She sat beside him. Everyone else was watching the big game, but Dane couldn't care less about football. All he could think about was Gabrielle and the haunted look in her eyes.

Dane's only reply to Nana was a grunt.

"Why aren't you in there doing something?" Nana asked. "Carry her off to Vegas. I'll watch the baby."

"Nana, I'm afraid it's a little more complicated than that. Ben is Jack's father. Don't you think it'd be just a tad dishonorable for me to try breaking up a family?"

"You and your damned honor," Nana said. From out of her coat pocket, she withdrew a cigar and proceeded to snip off the end, light it and take a big puff.

"What're you doing?" Dane said, taking it away from her and stomping it out. "Are you trying to do yourself in?"

"That's what I'm talking about," she said, calmly

taking another cigar from her pocket. "You've always had this overinflated sense of justice when half the things you're judging are none of your business."

Dane started to speak, but she cut him off.

"I'm nearly triple your age, yet you think you can tell me whether or not I'm allowed to smoke a good cigar. That's BS."

What a day this was turning out to be. Dane had already lost Gabrielle and Jack, and now his Nana had turned into a cussing, smoking teen. "I'm thinking that new boyfriend of yours is a bad influence."

"He's the best thing to happen to me in twenty years." She took a deep puff off her cigar, blowing a perfect smoke ring. "Now, back to you. I've seen you and Gabrielle together and you have chemistry. Have you kissed her?"

Dane pleaded the Fifth.

"You have! I knew it."

Cringing, Dane figured it was time to head back inside, but he said, "Whether or not we've shared a few intimacies is irrelevant."

"Don't pull out those big words with me, Dane Brain. I don't care how smart you are, at the moment, you're being pretty damned dumb." The sweet cigar smoke was starting to give him a headache. Or maybe it was his grandmother's language.

"Nana, look, I handle cases of broken families all the time. When I thought Ben could be permanently out of the picture, there might've been a chance for me and Gabrielle. But now that he's back, I refuse to come between them. Jack needs his mother and father. End of story."

TWO WEEKS PASSED, AND DURING Tuesday-night bath time with Jack, Gabby realized she'd forgotten to grab his hooded turtle towel from the dryer.

"Ben!" When a few minutes passed without him coming, she hollered again.

"What's up?" he asked, taking his iPod headphones out of his ears.

She explained what she needed, and he was off.

He returned with not only the ultrasoft infant towel she'd requested, but all of the other towels that'd been in the dryer. While she finished washing Jack's hair, Ben folded the towels and then tucked them under the sink.

"Thanks," she said, rinsing Jack's hair.

"You know I can do more around here to help out. Especially with the baby."

She nodded.

"Gab." He knelt beside her at the tub, lightly splashing Jack. "Ever since I've been back, I get the sense you want nothing to do with me. I'm trying here. I know I hurt you, and I'm sorry a million times over, but I can't do this on my own. You have to meet me halfway."

Swallowing hard, she nodded.

"I love you, babe. I was a fool for leaving you, but I can't erase the past."

"I know," she said, taking Jack from the warm bath and wrapping him in his towel. "And I am trying. But you hurt me. I needed you, and you weren't there." Cradling their son against her chest, she stood. "Do you have any idea how scary that was for me? You know I don't have any family, and—"

He stood, too, and, bracing her face with his hands,

he kissed her slow and sweet. "I'm sorry. Please forgive me. Let me be your family."

"I want to, Ben, but I'm scared. What if you leave again?"

"I won't. Let's get married. I'll get a steady job. I'll become whoever you want me to be."

Turning her back on him, she went to the nursery to lotion, diaper and clothe her son. *Her* son.

"Gabby, talk to me." Ben stood behind her, curving his hands over her shoulders.

"I just need space, okay? I mean, I don't hear from you in months, and then all of a sudden you're back, acting as if nothing ever happened."

He stepped away and sat in the rocker.

Gabby finished with Jack, then kissed the sleepy baby before slipping him into his crib. Signaling for Ben to follow, she left the nursery to curl up on the far corner of the living room sofa.

Ben took the armchair across from her.

She wasn't sure where to start, so she jumped straight to the heart of their troubles. "Ben…while you were gone everything changed for me. I still love you, but in a different way."

A muscle ticked in his jaw. "This have anything to do with my brother?"

"No. Why can't you accept the fact that you messed up? Dane only cleaned up your mess. And I was a mess, Ben. My pregnancy was tough. I was sick all of the time. And then when I was put on bed rest, I had no one to turn to but your brother."

"Mama would've taken you in. She loves you." He

rose to sit beside her and take her hand in his. "Remember how amazing we used to be? How we'd stay up all night laughing over strip Monopoly? How I talked you into taking a sick day during the last big snow, so that we could make his and her snowmen. We used to cook together and throw parties and—"

"Stop," Gabby said, yanking her hand free to cover her ears. She knew it was juvenile, but she wanted him to quit sugarcoating what he'd done. "I just need time, okay?" Hands fisted on her lap, she struggled to find the right words. "For now, I'm committed to us trying to get back to the way we were, but I can't make you any promises."

"Fair enough. But you will try?" He took her hand again, unclenching her fingers, tenderly tracing the lines on her palm.

"Of course. For Jack."

"I want more," he said, "I want you to want me for you. We shared something special. We can make a fresh start."

More than anything, Gabby longed for just such a thing, only she feared she didn't want it with Ben, but with his big brother.

Chapter Fourteen

"This is wrong," Dane said, sliding into the black leather booth seat across from Gabrielle. She'd called him the previous night, asking him to meet her and the baby for lunch at a downtown steakhouse. The lighting was intimate, booths compartmentalized—like miniature rooms. The place, with its mahogany-paneled walls, white-clothed tables and antique brick floors was a favorite among the courthouse crowd. The tantalizing scent of fresh-grilled steaks didn't hurt, either. Dane had wanted to turn Gabrielle down, but he wasn't strong enough.

"What's wrong with two friends sharing a meal?"

"Are we *just* friends?"

She looked to Jackson, who was sleeping in his carrier. Fussing with his blanket, tucking it just so about his tiny feet, she said, "I don't know how to say this, so I'm going to just come out with it. I'm trying so hard to make things work with Ben, but that scares me. If I love him, why does being with him feel like work?"

"Wish I had an answer for you," he replied, his heart shattering.

Leaning forward, her hands tightly clasped on the table, she asked, "How is it we're this supposedly perfect little family when Ben's kisses feel flat to me? Our conversations dull? I want to make things work between us, but you're in the way. Only, that's stupid because Ben's the man I'm supposed to be with."

Her words sliced through him. To try exorcising Gabrielle from his system, Dane had gone on a date with a fellow judge. Five minutes in, he'd wanted out. The whole thing had felt sour.

"Say something. You're acting like the old you. You're like a stone—cold and unyielding."

"You're being ridiculous," he said, glaring at the menu. "I'm the same as I've always been."

"Are you? Then how come you won't smile at me, or even look at our baby?"

He swallowed the wrong way on a gulp of water. After an awkward coughing fit, he managed to say, "Yes, I put a lot of time into making sure you and the baby were healthy, but that doesn't give me any legal right to him. We've been over this."

"I'm not talking about legalities, Dane. I miss my friend," Gabrielle said in a forceful whisper. "Do you even remember the first time you experienced Jack kick? How you held your hand on my stomach and we watched him move around?"

"Of course I remember, but what does that have to do with anything? Ben's back. He wants you and his son. End of story. Now, where's the damned waitress? I need to get back to court."

The waitress came and went. Dane ordered a

French dip and iced tea. Gabby got a Reuben and stuck with her water.

"I want to hold him," Dane said, nodding toward her baby boy. He wanted to pretend, if only for a moment, he was Jack's father. During the time he'd been with Gabby, there was so much Dane had looked forward to. He'd wanted to share in first smiles and crawling. Eating solid foods and walking.

Without saying a word, Gabrielle scooped Jackson from his carrier and passed him over the table into Dane's outstretched arms.

How long Dane had wanted to hold the baby boy, but Ben had always been near. He didn't want his brother bearing witness to what would undoubtedly be an emotional time. Jackson's weight was slight against his chest, yet he radiated warmth. His smell was intoxicating. Like baby lotion and powder and everything innocent and good. Tears stung Dane's eyes.

"Look…" he said, nuzzling Jack's feathery hair "Gabrielle, my time with you was some of the happiest in my life. Had Ben not returned—with your blessing— I'd be living with you and Jack now. My house is cold and lonely. There's no color. No sound. No heart. I'm losing my mind without you—not a good thing for a judge." His flashed smile was wry.

"Oh, Dane…" Her face radiated good health and beauty, but also sadness. "I had no idea."

"Well…it's not something I broadcast. I feel like a freakin' nut case."

"Then you're in good company. I'm the same." Bowing her head, she covered her face with her hands. "I promised Ben that for Jack's sake, I would at least try making things work between us, but I don't know if I can."

"You can and will," Dane said, by instinct, rubbing Jack's back. "Months ago, you couldn't stop singing Ben's praises. Telling me about his guacamole and margaritas. How much you adore his grin."

"I never said I *adore* it. I mean, he's handsome, but…" Blushing furiously, she ducked her gaze.

"I know," he teased, "nobody compares to me, right?"

Groaning, she said, "I'd laugh about that if I weren't so afraid it was the truth."

"Hey…" Clutching Jack snugly against him, Dane switched to Gabrielle's side of the booth. Cupping his hand to her cheek, stroking her with his thumb, he said, "Truly, we're going to be great. You and Ben are going to fall into your old happy routine. I'll find some staid lady lawyer who's just as dull as me, and—"

"You're not dull," she said, covering his hand with hers. "You're funny and warm and spoiled me rotten."

"So that's the whole truth?" He nudged her shoulder. "You just want your own personal manservant back."

"It was a pretty sweet deal." Sighing, she rested her head on his shoulder.

"Your new start with Ben will be, too." Dane kissed Gabrielle's forehead, hoping he'd find some kind of distraction for himself. A hobby. A dog.

The tears pooling in her eyes physically hurt him. Why, while Ben had still been gone, hadn't Dane hired a justice of the peace to come marry them in her bedroom? They could've had a lavish ceremony later. All that would've mattered was Dane getting his ring on her finger. He'd been so worried about not hurting Ben that he hadn't stopped to consider he was also hurting himself, and, more important, Gabrielle.

ON WEDNESDAY MORNING, Gabby was folding a load of clothes when Ben ambled into the laundry room.

"Hey, beautiful," he said, kissing the side of her neck. She'd always been ticklish in the spot, which he full well knew.

"Stop," she said with an automatic giggle.

"Used to be you wouldn't want me to."

Sighing, she ignored his loaded statement in favor of folding her favorite long-sleeved red T-shirt. "Is Jack still sleeping?"

"Last time I checked."

"Which was when?" She sidestepped around him to grab a pile of clothes to take to her room.

"I don't know. Ten minutes, maybe?" He trailed after her.

On the way to her bedroom, she stopped off in the nursery. Jack was zonked out on his back. His lips made the sweetest suckling motion that made him look all the more adorable.

In her bedroom, while Ben sprawled across her bed, she put away her clothes.

She'd nearly finished when he said, "What do you think about having a party Saturday?"

"What's the occasion?" She turned off her closet light and shut the door.

"There's a night game at War Memorial and it's being televised." War Memorial was the Razorbacks' stadium in Little Rock. Though not nearly as big as the main campus's field in Fayetteville, opponents always felt the heat from the fans' famous hog calls.

"Who all do you want to invite?" Dane? the butterflies in her stomach hoped.

"I was thinking our old crowd. And Olivia and Stephanie if you'd like."

"What about Dane?" She tried sounding casual, as if just saying his name didn't mean so much.

Ben made a face. "He's not exactly the life of any party."

"That's not true," Gabby argued. "Dane's a lot of fun."

Sighing, Ben pressed the heels of his hands into his closed eyes. "You're killing me here, Gab. I know for whatever reason you're crushing on my brother, and it's got to stop. We're a couple. What don't you get about that fact?"

"Correction," Gabby said, "we *were* a couple. I'm not crushing on Dane. He's my friend. You and I are two strangers living together, trying to raise a child."

"Oh—that makes me feel welcome." Sitting up, he smacked his palm against the wrought-iron footboard. "You promised you'd give us a try, but from what I can tell, you just don't give a damn."

Lips pressed tight, arms folded across her chest, Gabby did a mental count to ten.

"Is your silence the same as an admission?"

"Give it a rest," she pleaded. "After you left, I had to learn how to live without you. I didn't even know where you were, let alone if you were ever coming back. You didn't call, didn't write, yet you're acting as if just because I had your baby that gives you a hold on me."

She stood near enough for him to reach out and stroke her arm. Softening his tone, he said, "I thought we were forgetting the past nine months and starting over."

"W-we are." Her voice cracked. "But you're expecting too much from me too fast. You don't have a clue how rough the past months have been. I can't even imagine returning to work in just three weeks. Moreover, you don't seem to care what I've been through. Now, this is my house, and Dane is my friend. If we're hosting a party, he will be on the invitation list."

Snorting, Ben said, "He probably won't come."

"That's his prerogative."

SATURDAY NIGHT, DANE STOOD on Gabrielle's front porch, ringing the doorbell as if he were a stranger. He resented the hell out of being put in this position. But he apparently didn't resent it that much, or he wouldn't have even come.

"You made it," Gabrielle said, tossing her arms around him for a hug. "Mmm...I'm so happy to see you. Olivia and Stephanie aren't here yet, and most everyone else is a friend of Ben's."

For just an instant, while holding Gabrielle in his arms, Dane had felt whole again, but then she'd let him go.

From inside came a raucous group cheer. Apparently, the Razorbacks had scored.

Gabrielle winced at the noise.

"Where's Jack?" Dane asked.

"On Ben's lap. He bought him a baby Hog warm-up suit, hat and socks." Bowing her head, she said, "He looks cute."

It had been a beautiful fall day and the temperature was still in the midsixties. Seeing how the crowd gathered around the TV was oblivious to him and Gabrielle even being there, Dane took her hand, leading her to the porch swing. "Talk to me. You look sad."

Seated beside him, she shrugged. "I'm all right. Exhausted, but otherwise fine."

Liar. Her eyes were red and her complexion pale.

She'd put her hair in two loose braids that framed her face. He wanted to take hold of them, drawing her in for a kiss.

Trying to get his mind on something other than her lips, he asked, "How's Ben's job hunt going?"

"Okay, I guess. He has a couple of good corporate leads, and was offered a job selling Fords at a friend's car lot. With his people skills, I can see where he'd probably be good at it—selling cars."

"No doubt," Dane said, not bothering to hide a sarcastic chuckle.

"At least he's trying," Gabrielle said a little defensively.

"So I take it things are going good between you?"

"No. Things are more comfortable between us, but Ben's still in the guest room if that's what you mean."

"Sorry," he said, hoping to dispel the anger flashing in her eyes. "Whatever you do with my brother is your business. I didn't mean to imply—"

"Stop." She gently pressed her fingers to his lips, shooting an erotic jolt through him. "For Jack's sake, you were the one encouraging me to reunite with Ben, remember?"

Of course he remembered, but he didn't have to like it. The thought of any other man touching her was inconceivable. Ben touching her? That thought sent Dane over the edge every night.

"I'm good," she said, "and I want you to be, too."

He touched his forehead to hers. "I shouldn't have come."

"Why? Dane, there's no law against us being friends."

He nodded. Trouble was, he wanted so much more than friendship from her.

Gabrielle took Dane inside. She put a bottled beer in his hand, steering him toward the sofa. Stephanie and Olivia finally arrived, wearing matching "Future Hog" maternity shirts with arrows pointing toward their baby bumps. The Razorbacks won their play-off game. Everyone was jubilant—except him. He tried getting into the spirit of the night, but nothing worked.

Ben was constantly jiggling the baby on his knee. It was a wonder the kid didn't puke. Gabrielle asked him to stop, and to Ben's credit he did—for a little while. But then he was back at it.

Gabby stepped in and took the infant, huddling in the kitchen with Olivia and Stephanie. Dane thought about joining them, but just retreating to his quiet house sounded like a better plan. But then he got cornered by an old friend, and talked stocks for the better part of an hour.

Gabrielle had long since put Jackson to bed, so before heading home for the night, Dane let himself into the nursery, closing the door behind him. Save for a night-light, the room was dark. Just enough moonlight crept through the curtains he'd helped hang to silhouette Jack's perfect sleeping form.

Bracing his arms on the side of the crib, drinking in the sight of the tiny miracle that'd been growing inside Gabrielle, Dane couldn't help but wonder if Ben even appreciated what he had.

The door opened, and Gabrielle put her hands to her chest. "Dane. Jeez, everyone thought you'd gone home."

"Should've," he said, skimming Jack's crazy soft hair.

"He's gorgeous, isn't he?" Standing alongside him, she said, "I can't get enough of this little guy." Grabbing the edge of the baby's fleece blanket, she tucked it under his left foot, which had been sticking out. "Of course, when he wakes at about three in the morning, I'll probably have other thoughts."

"Does Ben ever take turns with you when it comes to late-night feedings?"

"He's tried, but it's kinda tough, seeing how I'm breast-feeding."

"I suppose." Tough, but not impossible. Dane had done considerable reading on the subject, and it was no big deal for the mother to express milk for times when she wasn't available. "Have you figured out a plan for when you go back to the spa?"

"I'm going to try taking Jack with me, but if that doesn't work, your mother offered to help." Leaving the baby, she strode to the rocker and had a seat. "My feet are on fire."

"That was nice."

"Having my feet burst into flames?" she teased. Lord,

she was a sight to behold. Hair an adorable mess, just the way he liked it. Smile sassy, yet at the same time sweet.

"I was talking about my mom."

"I know." Closing her eyes, she rocked. Outside of the nursery, the party wound on. Hard rock pulsed through the walls. "It's a miracle Jack's sleeping through all of this."

"When is everyone leaving?"

Sighing, she said, "Who knows? Maybe I'll just take a cue from my son and drag myself off to bed."

"Want me to carry you?" Though he'd meant the question to be a joke, it didn't come out sounding that way. When her smile faded, he said, "Sorry, I…"

"You have nothing to apologize for." Easing her fingers into the hair at her temples, she asked, "You ever wonder how we got to this place? I mean, me with Ben, you on your own? It doesn't feel right. Like I'm going through the motions of life, but not really living."

Boy, did that sound familiar. "It'll get better," he said. "A couple of times tonight, you and my brother looked cozy."

"Jealous?" Even in the shadows, he felt her stare.

Hell, yes.

Licking her lips, she said, "I'm sorry. That was inappropriate."

He couldn't disagree.

Angling his head back, he tried working the kinks from his neck, but no such luck. He feared they were becoming a permanent fixture. "I've been thinking lately about resigning. Taking a position with a Little Rock law firm. A friend of mine from college has offered me a partnership. All I have to do is say the word, and it's a done deal."

"But you love being a judge."

"It's all right." With a sad laugh, he shook his head. *Too damned bad I love you more.* Because he loved her, he wanted her to do the right thing—and stay with Ben so that Jackson grew up with his true father.

Chapter Fifteen

A week after her last conversation with Dane, Gabby still had a tough time forgetting the hurt in his eyes. Her asking if he was jealous of his brother had been unconscionable. She'd meant it as a lighthearted quip. An auto-response. Never had she meant to hurt him—or herself. It no longer mattered that Dane had become an integral part of her life. She was now a parent, and as such, Jackson's needs came above her own.

Then you're admitting you miss Dane far more than you should?

No. She'd made Ben a promise to work things out between them, and for their baby's sake, she would.

Speaking of Ben, she heard him stirring. The sound of the wood floor creaking in the hall. The bathroom taps going on and then off.

Drawing the covers over her head, she tried not to focus on all of the times she'd listened in on Dane's morning routine.

Minutes later, Ben was at her door. "I was talking with my friend Craig and we're going to the Cotton Bowl. Does that work for you?"

"Sure," she said, actually a little relieved he'd be gone. "Where are you getting the money?"

He shrugged. "I've still got a few bucks saved from those commercials I did in L.A."

"What about your job leads? Did any pan out?"

Sitting at the foot of her bed, he said, "None of them really worked for me. I'm thinking about going back to school. Maybe learning a trade. My friend Matt pulls down five Gs a month welding."

After taking a moment to let that sink in, Gabby said, "Let me get this straight. You have a perfectly good business degree, yet because you don't *like* any of the jobs you've applied for, you're giving up the search?"

"You're getting it all wrong. And might I add," he said with one of his trademark sexy grins, "that you're looking particularly fetching this morning in those pink pj's."

"Ben," she blurted, "what's wrong with you? You won't even try being an adult. Why can't you just accept the fact that you're not a kid anymore? You have responsibilities."

"Aw, baby," he said, lying down next to her, smoothing her hair. "Don't be mad. I'm sorry, okay? I'll table trade school for now, and just take the car sales job, all right?"

Groaning, she stared at the ceiling. "I don't even know what to say to you. The whole reason we're trying to make things work between us is so that Jack grows up with a father, but you're more like a younger brother. Last weekend's party got way out of hand. You've been here weeks and still don't have a job. You hardly help out at all around the house. Tell me, why should I bother keeping you here, because honestly, you cause me more work than pleasure."

"If it's pleasure you need," he said in a suggestive tone, "then I'll be happy to—"

"Just be quiet!" Tossing back her comforter, she stormed out of her room, adding on her way, "And after that, grow up."

Unfortunately, Ben followed. "I get it, okay? You're right, I haven't done much around here to help you out, and I'm sorry." Grabbing her arm just before she entered the nursery, he pulled her into a hug. "I know I should get my act together. Maybe you getting all fiery is the kick I needed." Kissing her cheek and the tip of her nose before moving to her lips, he whispered, "I love you. You're my *Fab Gab*."

The endearment transported her to a happier time when she'd loved Ben, too. Her life had seemed so carefree then. Like living one big party was a good thing. Now, since having Jack, yes, she still wanted to have fun, but in a different way.

"I—I'll give you another chance," she said, her palms against his chest, "but this is it. Once I'm back at work, I'm going to need help with Jack and cooking and laundry and scrubbing toilets. There's no way I can do all of it alone."

"I know," he said. "And I'm so sorry for ever thinking you could." After kissing her again, he said, "You'll see, from now on, I'm going to be a changed man."

"Is he doing better?" Olivia asked the Sunday afternoon before Gabby returned to the spa. They were indulging in a sinful brunch at a local teahouse that had been opened in a renovated Victorian house. All of the rooms were decorated in period style with plenty of antique case goods and tables covered in vintage lace cloths. The antique china didn't match, but provided a shabby-chic flair to go with the delicious homemade soups, sandwiches and pies. Dean Martin crooned familiar love songs. Over peach iced teas, Gabby had told her friend all of the promises Ben had made. It'd been a week since their talk, and to his credit, he had done a considerable amount of laundry—but only items that were easy to fold.

"He's great with washing towels, and always does the dishes, so yes, I suppose you could say he's much better."

"But…" Olivia, still a week out from her due date, leaned forward, absentmindedly stirring her tea.

"It's somehow still not enough." Jack slept in his carrier on the floor beside her. He looked so peaceful. Oblivious to his mother's emotional chaos.

"Because of your feelings for Dane?"

Gabby sharply looked up. "What feelings? Dane's my friend. I really am trying to be with Ben—for Jack's sake. It's the right thing to do."

"According to Dane, Ben or your own heart?"

"Congratulations!" Gabby said Tuesday morning, giving Stephanie a big hug. Jack was spending the morning with Mama Bocelli. Steph had carried her identical twin girls to full term, and they'd both weighed in at a whopping six pounds, three ounces. "Your babies are gorgeous."

"Thanks," Stephanie said. "It was a lot of work getting them here, though."

Gabby laughed. "That, I remember all too well." After setting two teddy bears and a balloon bouquet on the room's windowsill, she asked, "Do you need anything?"

"No, thanks. Lisa's been great. She just left a few minutes ago to take care of her family."

Sitting in the chair beside Steph's bed, Gabby said, "I'll bet it was nice having your coach for the delivery. You know, so everything went according to plan."

"It was, but that still didn't make it hurt any less." Brushing her riot of curls back from her face, she asked, "Was it really awful without Dane?"

"Who knows? I didn't end up using any of what we'd learned, so I suppose in that sense it wasn't what I'd expected. Plus, I missed Dane. We had a connection, you know? With Ben, it was like experiencing the most intimate moment imaginable—only with your ex."

"I'm sorry," Steph said. "I missed Michael, too. Don't get me wrong—Lisa was great, but like you said about Dane, it just wasn't the same."

"Listen to us." Gabby forced a smile. "We're supposed to be celebrating, not sitting here commiserating." She stood and tidied Steph's array of flowers and other gifts. "Tell me what's the first thing you're going to do now that you're not pregnant."

"Mmm…I'm craving a nice glass of merlot."

Laughing, Gabby said, "Sounds good. I'll bring you a bottle."

"Bless you." Once Steph had stopped laughing, too, she said, "So, back to Ben. What are you going to do? Kick him to the curb, or try molding him into the man you need him to be?"

"Ugh. That's a question I ask myself at least fifty times a day. In fact—"

A knock sounded on the door. "Everyone decent?"

"Come in!" Steph sang out.

Gabby's pulse sped up as she saw Dane strolling through the door, part of his face hidden by a dozen yellow roses.

"Congrats," he said, setting the flowers on Stephanie's nightstand before giving her a hug. "You did Michael proud. Those girls are already heartbreakers."

Tearing, Steph said, "Thank you. I hope he's smiling down on them."

"He is." Gabby covered her friend's hand with hers.

A nurse bustled in with one baby in a clear plastic cart. "Someone's hungry."

"That's my cue to leave," Dane said, reddening. He gave Steph another hug. "You did good."

"Thank you." She wiped away tears. Laughing, she said, "I can't stop crying."

"That's normal," the nurse said, handing over the baby. "Your hormones are going haywire."

"I guess," Steph said, while Gabby leaned in for a closer look at the fitful newborn. "I can't wait for us all to have playdates."

"That will be fun," Gabby agreed.

"I don't mean to rush you," the nurse said, "but our mom has another wailer waiting in the nursery."

Gabby made her goodbyes and left with Dane holding open the door.

Out in the hall, he said, "Long time, no see. How have you been?"

"Good," she managed to say, even though her mouth was dry. Just standing near him was a treat. His citrus-and-leather aftershave acted as an aphrodisiac. She wanted to wrap him in a hug and never let go.

He nodded. "Me, too. Want to grab a cup of coffee?"

"Love to."

With its fluorescent lights and beige walls, the hospital cafeteria wasn't big on ambience, but seated across from Dane, Gabby didn't need candlelight to put her in a happy mood. Even though they were surrounded by scrub-wearing employees and other visitors, for Gabby, no one existed but him.

"Where's the baby?" he asked, stirring two sugars into his cup.

"With your mom."

He winced. "Poor kid."

"Oh, stop," she scolded. "Your mother's wonderful. A little bit of a buttinski, but otherwise great."

"What'd she do?" He sipped his coffee.

"Just grilled me about how things are going with Ben." Gabby added cream and diet sweetener to her coffee.

"And…how are *things?*"

"Better," she said, wrapping both hands around her cup. The hospital was chilly, and the coffee's warmth was soothing. "He's trying hard to be everything I need him to be."

"Which is?" He raised his eyebrows.

"A little more grown-up." She wouldn't give him the satisfaction of admitting she wanted his little brother to be more like him.

"Mmm-hmm. Good luck."

"YOU'RE GETTING PRETTY GOOD at that," Nana said to Ben, hovering over him while he changed Jackson's diaper.

Dane watched from his mother's living room sofa. Mama had set up a portable crib and changing table in Pops's den.

"Thanks," Ben said, beaming under Nana's praise. Finished snapping Jackson's tiny jeans, he scooped him up, flying him through the air.

"Quit that," Nana said. "You'll drop him on his head, and then he won't see right."

Dane had to laugh at his grandmother's logic.

Gabrielle was in the kitchen with Mama, helping her clean up. He'd offered, but Mama wouldn't hear of it, claiming it'd been too long since she and Gabrielle had had a nice chat. Dane couldn't imagine how traumatic that must be. A part of him wanted to rescue her, another part wanted to forget he'd ever met her. Before Gabrielle, his life may have been predictable and routine, but at least he hadn't been consumed with constant *what-ifs*.

What if he'd gone against his every belief concerning right and wrong and just plunged into a relationship with her? Would he be content with his decision? Or eaten by regrets? Would his family hate him for destroying his little brother's life?

"Here," Ben said, plopping Jackson onto Dane's lap. "Hold him for a sec. I need to help Mama and Gab with the dishes."

"Mom doesn't want help," Dane said.

Ben patted Dane's shoulder. "You might be older than me, but you've got a lot to learn about women, big bro. Trust me, when a woman tells you she doesn't want you washing dishes, she's lying." He walked to the kitchen whistling.

All this time, Pops had been watching football from his recliner. "When are you going to stand up to Ben?"

"Excuse me?"

Looking him straight in the eyes, Dane's father said, "Judging by the way that baby's mother is always looking at you, I'd say Benny is the one needing help reading the ladies." Dane's father had always been a man of few words, so to hear him throw in his two cents on a matter Dane didn't think anyone had even noticed aside from himself and Gabrielle left him off balance.

"I'm not following you," Dane said, nuzzling Jackson's sweet-smelling hair.

"Don't play dumb with me. Any fool can see you're lusting after Benny's girl. Too bad for him, out of his own stupidity, it's no longer your brother she wants." Holding out his arms, his dad added, "Give me that kid. Your mom and Nana are all the time hogging him."

Dane did as his father asked, then wandered into the kitchen. He felt like a stranger in his childhood home. As if he didn't know what to do or say.

"Check it out, Mama." Ben wowed them with his dish-drying skills. "Look at what Gab taught me how to do."

"Impressive," his mother said.

"If you're a nine-year-old," Nana said with a snort.

"Give him some credit," Gabrielle said, turning Dane's stomach when she rubbed Ben's back. "When I first met him, he ate on nothing but paper plates. Now he not only eats off china, but uses genuine silverware, too."

Laughing, Ben slipped his arm around her shoulders. His motion was easy, natural, and it irked the hell out of Dane.

"I'm impressed," Mama said to Gabrielle. "You've accomplished in a few weeks what it took me years to try to teach him. Thank you."

"No problem." She now had her arm around Ben's waist. And just like that, they were a couple again. It might have been rough going in the beginning, but they would make it work. Effectively sealing Dane's fate to live the rest of his life without Gabrielle or her son.

GABRIELLE HAD BEEN BACK at the spa for two days, and already she was exhausted. She could've stayed home longer with Jackson, but having taken off so much time before having him, she felt honor-bound to head back early. Making matters worse was the fact that long-overdue Olivia had finally had her baby. It'd been a particularly rough delivery, ending in an emergency C-section. Gabby hadn't felt comfortable leaving until she'd been assured Olivia and her son would be fine. By the time she and Ben had left the hospital, it'd been after 3:00 a.m.

Dane and Stephanie had also been there, but upon seeing Gabby with Ben, Dane hadn't stayed for very long, asking Stephanie to call him should there be trouble. It bothered Gabby that he'd left. That he didn't so much as say hello to her. That the last time they'd shared Sunday dinner at his parents', he'd looked at her with disdain. And that had broken her heart.

Her private massage room featured an aquamarine glass-tile floor, with three walls painted to resemble a serene coral reef, complete with fish and an octopus peeking out of a crag in the trompe l'oeil rocks. The fourth wall was glass gazing out on an oriental water garden. While the massage table occupied the room's center, comfy rattan seating and fluffy white area rugs softened the space's edges.

During a break in her appointments, Gabby sat at her acrylic desk, needing to study online sales figures sent by her accountant. But instead, she leaned back in her white leather chair, staring out at the dreary day.

It resembled her mood.

She'd wanted Jack with her, but after one day with him at the spa, she'd known it wouldn't work. It wasn't good business to stop in the middle of a massage to change a diaper, and it wasn't good parenting not to be able to care for her son when he needed her. Meaning, since he was still out of a job, Ben was home caring for Jack, which was where Gabby wanted to be.

Before Jack had entered her world, her days at the spa had been highly satisfying, but now she missed her baby boy.

"How's it going?" the receptionist, Richard, asked. He was working his way through college, and had weathered his fair share of sexist jokes regarding his position.

"I'm pooped." Gabby thumped her forehead to her desk. "Is it five yet?"

"'Fraid not. And even if it were, I've got a question." He wagged the cordless phone, the mouthpiece of which he had covered. "Mrs. Benson is running late. Can you see her at five-thirty?"

Groaning, Gabby asked, "Any chance of you telling the mayor's wife that I've been abducted by aliens?"

"If you want, but considering she's one of your best clients and *generously* tips even *me* at Christmas, I'd love to tell her good news."

She glanced up. "But if aliens have me, surely she can't expect me to give her a massage?"

"Great," he said with a big grin, uncovering the phone. "Mrs. Benson, Gabby would be happy to fit you in whenever it's convenient."

Richard finalized details with the client as he left the room. Gabby swallowed a knot in her throat. She hadn't realized how much she hadn't missed working until returning to her job. Her breasts ached from not feeding Jack, and every bone in her body hurt from forcing her swollen feet into too-tight shoes.

Peeking his head back in, Richard asked, "Want me to make you some tea?"

"No, thanks." Trying to ignore the throbbing center of her forehead, she grabbed for the thick envelope from her accountant.

"Okay, but Christmas bonus time is coming. Don't forget I offered." He winked.

She threw a paper clip at him as he jogged back to his station at the spa's posh reception area.

Somehow, Gabby made it through the day. At five, she called Ben, telling him she'd be home late. He told her no problem, even though for her, it was a very big problem. She'd tried expressing her milk, but her breasts still hurt—bad.

Making small talk during Mrs. Benson's session felt endless, as did her short commute home.

When she entered the house, she kicked off her pink Crocs, dumped her purse, keys and accountant's notes on the entry-hall table. "Ben?"

Suddenly Gabby realized Jackson was crying.

Figuring Ben must be in the bathroom or napping, Gabby made a mad dash for the nursery. Jack sounded frantic.

"Sweetie," she crooned, scooping him from his crib. "Mommy's here. Shhh…" She tried soothing him, but his diaper had soaked through to his jammies and he was sopping wet.

She made quick work of changing his diaper and dressing him in clean, dry clothes. That calmed him, but judging by his cry, he was also hungry.

Where in the hell was Ben?

With Jack clutched to her chest, she sat in the rocker, quickly unbuttoned her blouse and unlatched her maternity bra. Jack rooted and then furiously suckled, his little fist grabbing her aching left breast. When the pain of engorgement had subsided, she switched Jack to her right breast. Relief swept through her, as well as exhaustion.

"Ben?" she called. Was he sleeping? Hurt?

Once Jack had satisfied his hunger, he promptly fell asleep. She fumbled with closing her bra flaps, then pulled together her blouse.

Still cradling Jack, she searched the house for Ben, but found no sign of him. A quick check outside showed that his silver Dodge Charger was gone.

Chapter Sixteen

Assuming there had to have been an emergency for Ben to leave Jack on his own, Gabby's hands trembled so badly she had a hard time dialing Dane's cell.

He picked up on the third ring. "Gabrielle. What can I do for you?"

"Dane, something horrible must've happened to Ben." She relayed how she'd found Jack crying and alone. "I'm not sure what to do. Should I call police or emergency rooms?"

"Hold off on that," Dane said. "Let me check a few of his favorite haunts."

"Like bars?" Anger at Dane's accusation seized her stomach. "Ben would never leave Jack home alone so that he could go out drinking."

"If you say so." Dane's tone was droll, as if he knew his brother so much better than she.

"Never mind," she snapped. "I shouldn't have even called you." Before he said something to upset her even further, she hung up.

Pacing the living room with Jack's head resting on

her shoulder, Gabby alternately worried and fumed. After calling Mama Bocelli and discovering there was no emergency there, Gabby had called the hospital, but no one matching Ben's description had been admitted.

When he'd first returned, Gabby might have thought him capable of just up and taking off, but not now. Lately, he'd been a changed man—just like he'd promised. While she couldn't say she'd completely forgiven him for leaving her when she'd most needed him, she'd at least remembered why she'd first fallen for him—his infectious laugh and knack for turning most anything into fun. The new Ben, who'd finally figured out grown-ups couldn't have fun 24/7, was starting to grow on her.

An agonizing hour later, a key turned in her front door. In walked Ben, smiling as usual. "Hey, you finally made it home." Tweaking Jack's nose, he said, "Hey to you, too, little man. Have a good nap?"

Fury didn't begin to describe the anger surging through her. "Where have you been?"

He kissed her cheek before taking off his coat, slinging it over a kitchen bar stool. "Craig called. Wanted me to join him and a few other guys for a quick beer. I wasn't going to go, but he said he might have a lead on a great job, and Jack was zonked, so I figured since you were already on the way home, I should go for it."

Getting as far away from Ben as the living room allowed, she said, "You need to leave."

"Aw, baby, don't be mad." He approached her for a hug, but she slipped out of reach.

"When I got home, Jack was frantic. Any idiot knows

that you never leave an infant alone—even if Craig calls, wanting you to play."

"But, baby, it was about a job. You want me to land something that pays major coin, right?"

Fists clenched, it was all she could do to keep her voice calm so as not to upset Jack. "You're a fool. Our child could've been in serious trouble, yet you don't even care."

"Of course I do," he reasoned. "I love the kid. But I also love being able to provide for my family."

He still didn't grasp the gravity of what he'd done. "How long was Jack alone?"

"Hardly any time at all. Maybe an hour or two—tops."

She laughed, lacing her tone with plenty of sarcasm. "In my book, ten minutes is too long, yet you thought nothing of leaving our child alone for more than an hour?" Pacing again, holding on to Jack for dear life, thanking God that he hadn't been seriously hurt, she said, "You're never going to change. Why can't you be more like Dane?"

Ben's expression became thunderous. "Oh—so that's the real problem." He gave a harsh laugh. "I knew the second I found out he'd helped himself to my house and pregnant woman that he—"

"Whoa. This stopped being your house when you abandoned *your* pregnant woman. As for Dane, he's done nothing but try to fix the mess you made. Honestly, I don't know how I would've made it through my pregnancy without him."

"Story of my life," Ben said, sitting on the sofa, defensively crossing his arms. "Dane's all too willing to charge to the rescue—even when his white knight routine isn't necessary."

"Do you realize how close I came to losing Jack? If it hadn't been for Dane actually moving in here to help, we might not have a baby to be fighting over."

"You know what?" Ben said, shaking his head while giving her a glare. "If you're so enamored with my big bro, you should go for it. I'm tired of trying to live up to your impossible standards."

Glaring right back, she said, "Is it really so tough to just not leave our son home alone? If you needed to hang with your buddies so bad, I would've rather you took Jack to the bar with you."

"Look," he said, rising to his feet, "this is getting us nowhere. I'm sorry I went out with Craig. I never intended to put Jack in danger or tick you off. You think you're this model of motherhood perfection, but you have your own issues." Heading down the hall to his room, he called over his shoulder, "Ever stopped to think how much your being a constant downer must be affecting our son?"

Following him, she snapped, "It's called being a parent instead of just hanging out. You might try it sometime."

"No," he said, taking his suitcase from the closet. "I think I'll leave that to Dane, since it's obviously him you'd rather be with."

"Stop," Gabby snapped. "For just once in your life can't you accept the fact that you screwed up? This has nothing to do with Dane, and everything to do with you."

From the living room came the sound of the front door opening. "Gabrielle?" Dane called.

"Great," Ben said, shoving his few clothes into his bag. "Just what we need."

"I'm in the guest room!" Gabby shouted.

In two seconds, Dane was in the doorway. To his younger brother, he said, "I see you made it home."

"Don't start."

"Oh—I'm going to do far more than start. You need to wake up and take charge of your life."

"Trust me, big bro, I'm doing just that, starting by getting the hell out of here. Gab, I've tried so hard to be whoever you want me to be, but I'm done. My whole life I've been trying to live up to Dane's standards, but seeing how that's not good enough, peace out." Brushing past Gabby, he kissed the top of Jack's head. "As far as I'm concerned," he said on his way to the bathroom to shove his few toiletries into his bag, "you two deserve each other."

As abruptly as he'd reentered her life, Ben walked out the front door, slamming it behind him.

Trembling head to toe, Gabby sank onto the sofa, holding Jack for all she was worth. "I—I don't get it. How is it that he's the one who did something wrong, yet I'm the one feeling punished?"

Sitting beside her, Dane said, "Maybe because you've been putting up with Ben's stunts for so long that he's swaying you toward the dark side?" Nudging her shoulder, he laughed. "Seriously, one of these days, my kid brother will get a clue. Lucky for you, you're not going to have to wait for that far-off day."

"What's that mean?"

"What do you think?" Rolling his eyes, he took Jack

from her. "Just as soon as we can get a license, we'll be married. I want you to quit your job and focus all of your energies on keeping this guy in good shape."

After what she'd just been through with Ben, Gabby couldn't believe what she was now hearing. "Could you be any less sensitive or more controlling?"

He looked confused. "What do you mean? Remember back when you told me you might be falling for me? I thought being with me is what you wanted."

"Not like this—you telling me what I'm going to do." Exasperated, she stormed into the kitchen to pour a glass of wine. After taking a couple of gulps, she said, "I'm sick of you Bocelli men dictating my life. One minute, you're telling me you and I will never be together, that for Jack's sake, I should marry Ben. Now, just as my every instinct has been telling me all along, I discover Ben is the mess my queasy stomach told me he was, and suddenly, you're telling me you and I are getting married?"

"Gabrielle," he said, helping himself to a sip of her wine, "I didn't mean it like that. If you'd prefer, we can slow things down. Plan a fancy spring wedding."

"Haven't you heard a word I've said? Stop telling me what to do. I'm a grown woman, Dane, fully capable of making my own decisions. The first of which is sending you home."

IT WAS OFFICIAL—DANE WAS done with women.

The morning after Gabrielle told him off, Dane didn't just go for a morning jog, but more of a death run. She had some nerve, whining about how much she missed him, and then turning down his proposal. Granted, he could've been more suave, but still, in times of crisis, he believed in getting straight to the point. Nothing good ever came from pussyfooting around.

Finished with his run, he took a quick shower and put on his best suit and power tie. He was determined not to waste one more minute of his life thinking about Gabrielle. He took a couple of granola bars from his pantry, and then snatched his keys, wallet and briefcase, making it to the courthouse thirty minutes ahead of schedule.

The first case on his docket was a clean divorce. A pair of twenty-somethings who'd jumped into marriage way sooner than they should've. His second case was more complex, another divorce, but with hundreds of thousands' worth of divided assets.

His third case involved kids. Nothing irked him more than when parents saw fit to use their children as weapons. Especially troubling to Dane was the infant being held by an elderly woman in the gallery's second row. The infant looked about the same age as Jackson. Which reminded Dane of Gabrielle—not a good thing.

Two hours later, he'd reached a verdict and escaped to the calm of his chambers.

For all of his resolutions to clear his mind of Gabrielle, he was doing a rotten job. Granted, he could've waited to propose, but what would've been the point? Ben had officially made his choice, which had in turn given Dane permission to pursue Gabrielle for himself.

It'd been a black-and-white situation. What didn't she get about that fact?

The week droned on.

Making matters worse, his mother had ordered him over for a family dinner Friday night. He'd wanted the weekend to himself. Lord knew, he'd earned it.

"You're late," his mother said when he entered his parents' home a little past seven.

"Sorry," he said, kissing her cheek. "Traffic was a nightmare."

"It's okay." She urged him inside. "Hurry up, it's cold."

From the kitchen, Nana hollered, "Is that Gabby? She promised to fix me up with a hottie from her—" In the living room, she stopped, putting her hands on her hips. "Oh. It's you."

Kissing her cheek, as well, Dane said, "I love you, too, Nana."

"I still love you," Nana said, "but seeing how I dumped Edgar, I'm on the prowl for a new man."

"That's good, Nana. I wish you luck." To his mother, he said, "Why did you trick me into seeing Gabby?"

"There's no trick. I just thought you might want to see your mother." She'd adopted her woe-is-me tone she used when she wanted her Christmas decorations taken down from the attic and Pops had refused.

"Uh-huh." Dane sat on the sofa, nodding to his father, who was in his recliner, deeply engrossed in a football game.

The door opened and in walked Gabrielle, holding Jackson in his carrier. The second she caught sight of Dane, she tensed, backing a little toward the way she'd just come. "I didn't know he would be here," she said, not bothering to hide her displeasure.

Nana asked, "Did you bring the number for my new boyfriend?"

"I think I'm going to go," Dane said, rising from the couch.

"No, I will." Gabrielle was already turning for the door.

"Whatever you do," Pops grumbled, "take it out of here. I can't hear my game."

Nana sighed. "Can we please get back to my new boyfriend?"

"I've got an idea," Pops said, fishing his wallet out of his back pocket. "How about someone hand me my grandson, and I'll hand you some money to take this whole debate somewhere else."

"Great idea," Nana said, snatching bills from her son's hand. "Let's pick up my boyfriend on the way."

"You're staying right here," Mama said, taking the bills from Nana and giving them to Gabrielle. "Now, give me that baby and you and Dane be on your way. You have lots to talk about."

"We really don't." Staring the woman he loved right in her eyes, he said, "I asked her to marry me, let me be a father to her child, and she turned me down. I'm done." He kissed his mother and Nana on their cheeks again, and then walked out the door.

THE SECOND DANE LEFT, Gabby burst into tears. "He's awful," she said into Mama's warm hug. "I despise him."

"I know, honey. Which is why you're going to go after him." Mama pushed her back, keeping hold of Gabby's upper arms. "I've seen you two together, and I dare you to deny how much you love my older son."

Gabby bit the inside of her lower lip hard enough to draw blood.

"I can only imagine how he proposed, he—"

"Dane didn't ask me to marry him, he told me. Just like he told me we could *never* be together before Ben left me for the second time. What doesn't he get about the fact that I'm a big girl, fully capable of making my own decisions? And the truth of the matter is..." Covering her mouth with her hands, eyes tearing, she whispered, "I *do* love him."

"Of course you do," Nana said. "Which is why you're going to forgive his lack of romance finesse and remember how he makes up for it in areas of dependability."

WITH DANE'S PARENTS WATCHING Jack, Gabby steered her Jeep straight for Dane's house. It was a boxy, modern, glass-and-steel masterpiece she'd last visited with Ben. Located on top of the tallest hill in town, the view from his living room—and most every other nook and cranny—was breathtaking.

Pulling her car into his drive, her heart raced to a disturbing degree. Would he even want to talk to her? Could she blame him if he didn't?

At his front door, it took her a few minutes to gather her courage. The December night was chilly, yet even her shivering couldn't make her ring the bell. What if he turned down her proposal?

Like you did his?

Straightening her shoulders, Gabby forced herself to take the plunge.

It took her three rings before Dane opened the door.

And even then, his cold stare wasn't exactly welcoming. "May I help you?"

She swallowed the knot in her throat and charged past him into the house. The place hadn't changed. It had been professionally decorated, and even showcased in several local magazines and newspapers. Black leather sofas and chairs topped area rugs that were vibrant shades of red, royal blue and yellow. The floors were polished black concrete. The walls were white and held pricey works of modern art. Just as she remembered, floor-to-ceiling windows looked out on the world. The house was gasp-worthy, yet for all of its glory, the perfection of the place felt hollow. Like it didn't have a beating heart.

Helping herself to Dane's sofa, Gabby patted the cushion beside her. "Join me?"

"Thanks, but I'll stand."

She shrugged. "Whatever. I guess since you're obviously busy, I'll make this brief."

"Good."

She'd never seen Dane sulk, but considering how many times she'd pouted when they'd been living together, she guessed she had it coming. Licking her lips, she forced a deep breath and said, "I'm sorry. Very. A-and, if the offer still stands, I would love to marry you." Now that she was on a roll, after pausing for air, she rambled on. "I always thought you were the stubborn one, but in the end, it was me who loused things up. Anyway…" Wringing her hands on her lap, never had she felt more alone. Why wouldn't he say something? Did he really hate her that much? Had he already forgotten all of the special times they'd shared?

She was on the verge of giving in to tears when he crossed to her, kneeling in front of her and taking her hands. "I'm the one who's sorry. I should've brought flowers and candy and a ring. I should've—"

"Shh," she said before kissing him quiet. "Everything about you is perfect."

"True." His grin was contagious. "It's about time you reached that conclusion."

After giving him a playful pummeling, she pulled him onto the couch for a longer, more satisfying kiss. Once her craving for him had been momentarily sated and they'd gotten cozy lying side by side, she summoned the courage to ask, "You were so guilt-ridden about being with me. If we marry, are you sure you can handle it? You know, seeing Ben at family gatherings and such?"

Groaning, he said, "The second I heard my brother had left his own child home alone, all bets were off. If he doesn't even have the sense to care for an infant, then he sure as hell can't care for you." Pressing his lips to hers, he settled in for a leisurely exploration of her mouth.

"Hmm…haven't I been saying that ever since he stepped foot back into town? But who didn't listen?"

"I know, I know. Give me the next fifty or so years to make it up to you?"

Snuggling against him, thrilled that Jack and her were finally on the right track, she teased, "Make it sixty and we have a deal."

Epilogue

"Has anyone seen my teeth?" Nana lifted the train of Gabby's wedding dress, looking underneath.

"Honestly," Mama said, helping in the search, "I can't take you anywhere."

It was Christmas Day and Gabby couldn't think of a greater gift than her wedding day. Despite her gnawing uneasiness about the way they'd left things with Ben, she'd wanted to marry Dane as quickly as possible. She wanted to make it official before anything else could go wrong. Their wedding had been thrown together and was being held at the rambling Bocelli home. All of the living room furniture had been placed in temporary storage, making way for fifty chairs and a fragrant evergreen-and-poinsettia-adorned altar placed in front of the ornately carved, dark cherry fireplace. With a fire crackling in the hearth, despite sleet tinkling outside against the windows, the spirit inside was warm and happy.

Gabby, with Olivia and Steph's help, was getting ready for the most important day of her life in Mama and Pops's master bedroom. She stared at her reflection in the oversize cheval mirror, and happily approved of her gown and the magic her friends had worked with her hair.

"Thank you, guys." She pulled both into a group hug. "I never would've been able to throw this together on such short notice without you."

"Our pleasure," Olivia said, hugging her right back.

"Found 'em!" On all fours alongside the bed, Nana held up her dentures.

Shaking her head, Mama hustled Nana into the hall bathroom.

"Just think," Steph said. "In a few minutes, you'll be related to those two characters."

Gabby released a good-natured groan. All four of their babies were in Dane's childhood room, being watched by all six of the female Bocelli cousins. There were ten more boys, but they were in the sunroom, playing video games.

"Ready?" Olivia asked, adjusting Gabby's veil.

Forcing a deep breath and fanning her face, Gabby nodded. "I think so."

A knock sounded on the door and in walked the last person she'd expected to see on her wedding day—Ben. "Hey."

"Um, hi," Gabby said, looking to her bridesmaids for help.

Both looked away.

"Ladies," Ben said, "would you mind giving us a minute?"

Her friends looked to Gabby for permission to leave. Though her stomach was turning, she nodded.

Once they'd left, Ben shut the door behind them, then said, "Before you tie the knot with my brother, I wanted to apologize. I already spoke with him, but you..." A sad laugh escaped him. "We've shared a lot of good times. Lately, a lot of bad. And I'm sorry. You and my brother were right. I've got a lot of growing up to do."

"Why are you telling me this?" she asked, trying not to cry. The last thing she wanted was for her makeup to be ruined before she'd even walked down the aisle. "Why now?"

"Because I want you to know that I think you and Dane are perfect for each other. I wish you both a lifetime of happiness." He kissed her cheek, wiped tears from his own cheeks and then left the room.

Gabby had expected Ben to cause her trouble, but in reality, he'd put the crowning touch on her special day.

"You MAY NOW KISS THE BRIDE." Lifting Gabrielle's veil, Dane felt as if every dream he'd ever had had just come true.

"You're beautiful," he whispered before touching his lips to hers. She held Jackson in her arms, and he kissed the baby's forehead. "I love you both so much."

"We love you, too."

While the newlyweds kissed, family and friends cheered. The moment was made all the sweeter by the talk Dane had had with his brother. Not that he'd needed Ben's permission to do what he'd known was right in his heart, but his brother's blessing had been welcome.

Once they'd put sleepy Jackson to bed, greeted everyone in the receiving line, fed each other cake, shared dancing and champagne, Dane finally found a moment alone to be with his bride.

Slipping his arms around her waist, slow dancing with her in the privacy of his mother's laundry room, he said, "Are you aware, Mrs. Bocelli, that you've made me the happiest man alive?"

She kissed him. "Are you aware, Mr. Bocelli, that you've made me the happiest woman alive?"

He kissed her back. "So we're even?"

"Even Steven."

Turning to a reflective mood, he said, "This morning, I was thinking back to that Saturday I worked on Jack's changing table, how you said you wanted to throw a big party for his first Christmas. I'd say you succeeded."

"Thanks." She beamed.

From behind them came the sound of Olivia clearing her throat. "I, um, hate to break this up, but I have it on good authority that Gabby's some kind of love guru and just hooked up Nana."

"Could this wait until later?" Dane asked. "I'm kind of on the prelude to my honeymoon here."

Sighing, Olivia said, "Your flight to Tahiti doesn't leave until 5:00 a.m. Surely you can spare your bride for a few minutes."

"Tell you what," Gabrielle said to her friend, "how about you let me finish making out with my husband, and I'll see what I can do about hooking you up with one of the spa's hot male masseuses."

"Deal," Olivia said, "but don't take too long. All of this romance is making me crave a little of my own."

Once Gabrielle's friend had finally left them alone,

Nana poked her head in to let Gabrielle know she'd packed some of her favorite romance novels for Gabrielle to take on their honeymoon. After Nana, his mother wanted to know if he'd seen his father's universal remote.

After promising his mom that if he happened to find the remote he would rush it to his frantic father, Dane asked his bride, "Is this how our whole lives are going to be? Constantly interrupted by friends and family?"

"I hope so," Gabrielle said, squeezing him in a hug. "I love your family—and our friends. We're going to have an amazing life, you and me and Jack and whoever else might come along."

"You want to get started on that?" He punctuated his question with another kiss. "Making the *whoever else* portion of our family you just referred to?"

"Mmm…" On her tiptoes, nibbling his earlobe, she whispered in his ear, "I thought you'd never ask."

* * * * *

*Be sure to look for the next book in
Laura Marie Altom's* BABY BOOM *miniseries
coming in spring 2010, and find out if Olivia does
indeed get the romance she craves!*

In 2009 Harlequin celebrates
60 years of pure reading pleasure!

We're marking this occasion by offering
16 **FREE** full books to download and read.

Visit

www.HarlequinCelebrates.com

to choose from a variety of
great romance stories
that are absolutely **FREE!**

(Total approximate retail value of $60)

We invite you to visit and share the Web site
with your friends, family
and anyone who enjoys reading.

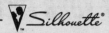

SPECIAL EDITION

FROM *NEW YORK TIMES*
BESTSELLING AUTHOR

SUSAN MALLERY

DESERT
ROGUES

THE SHEIK AND THE BOUGHT BRIDE

Victoria McCallan works in Prince Kateb's palace.
When Victoria's gambling father is caught cheating
at cards with the prince, Victoria saves her father from
going to jail by being Kateb's mistress for six months.
But the darkly handsome desert sheik isn't as harsh as
Victoria thinks he is, and Kateb finds himself attracted to
his new mistress. But Kateb has already loved and lost
once—is he willing to give love another try?

Available in October wherever books are sold.

SSE65481

Visit Silhouette Books at www.eHarlequin.com

REQUEST YOUR FREE BOOKS!

2 FREE NOVELS PLUS 2 FREE GIFTS!

HARLEQUIN®

American ★ *Romance*®

Love, Home & Happiness!

YES! Please send me 2 FREE Harlequin® American Romance® novels and my 2 FREE gifts (gifts are worth about $10). After receiving them, if I don't wish to receive any more books, I can return the shipping statement marked "cancel." If I don't cancel, I will receive 4 brand-new novels every month and be billed just $4.24 per book in the U.S. or $4.99 per book in Canada.* That's a savings of close to 15% off the cover price! It's quite a bargain! Shipping and handling is just 50¢ per book. I understand that accepting the 2 free books and gifts places me under no obligation to buy anything. I can always return a shipment and cancel at any time. Even if I never buy another book from Harlequin, the two free books and gifts are mine to keep forever.

154 HDN E4DS 354 HDN E4D4

Name _____ (PLEASE PRINT) _____

Address _____ Apt. # _____

City _____ State/Prov. _____ Zip/Postal Code _____

Signature (if under 18, a parent or guardian must sign)

Mail to the **Harlequin Reader Service:**
IN U.S.A.: P.O. Box 1867, Buffalo, NY 14240-1867
IN CANADA: P.O. Box 609, Fort Erie, Ontario L2A 5X3

Not valid to current subscribers of Harlequin® American Romance® books.

Want to try two free books from another line?
Call 1-800-873-8635 or visit www.morefreebooks.com.

* Terms and prices subject to change without notice. Prices do not include applicable taxes. N.Y. residents add applicable sales tax. Canadian residents will be charged applicable provincial taxes and GST. Offer not valid in Quebec. This offer is limited to one order per household. All orders subject to approval. Credit or debit balances in a customer's account(s) may be offset by any other outstanding balance owed by or to the customer. Please allow 4 to 6 weeks for delivery. Offer available while quantities last.

Your Privacy: Harlequin is committed to protecting your privacy. Our Privacy Policy is available online at www.eHarlequin.com or upon request from the Reader Service. From time to time we make our lists of customers available to reputable third parties who may have a product or service of interest to you. If you would prefer we not share your name and address, please check here. ☐

HAR09R2

From *New York Times*
bestselling authors

CARLA NEGGERS
SUSAN MALLERY
KAREN HARPER

More Than Words:
STORIES OF
STRENGTH

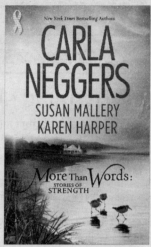

They're your neighbors, your aunts, your sisters and your best friends. They're women across North America committed to changing and enriching lives, one good deed at a time. Three of these exceptional women have been selected as recipients of Harlequin's More Than Words award. And three *New York Times* bestselling authors have kindly offered their creativity to write original short stories inspired by these real-life heroines.

Visit **www.HarlequinMoreThanWords.com**
to find out more, or to nominate
a real-life heroine in your life.

Proceeds from the sale of this book will be reinvested in Harlequin's charitable initiatives.

Available in March 2009 wherever books are sold.

SUPPORTING CAUSES OF CONCERN TO WOMEN
WWW.HARLEQUINMORETHANWORDS.COM

HARLEQUIN

PHMTW668

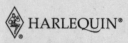